Lock Down  Presents

GET IT IN SLUGS

Love & Money

Written By

B. STALL

GET IT IN SLUGS | B. STALL

Copyright © 2024 B. Stall
GET IT IN SLUGS

All rights reserved. No part of this book may be reproduced in any form or by electronic or mechanical means, including information storage and retrieval systems without permission in writing from the publisher, except by a reviewer who may quote brief passages in review.

First Edition 2024

Printed in the United States of America

This is a work of fiction. Names, characters, places, and incidents either are products of the author's imagination or are used fictitiously. Any similarity to actual events or locales or persons, living or dead, is entirely coincidental.

Lock Down Publications
P.O. Box 944
Stockbridge, GA 30281
www.lockdownpublications.com

Like our page on Facebook: Lock Down Publications
www.facebook.com/lockdownpublications.ldp

Stay Connected with Us!

Text **LOCKDOWN** to 22828 to stay up-to-date with new releases, sneak peaks, contests and more…

Like our page on Facebook:
Lock Down Publications

Join Lock Down Publications/The New Era Reading Group

Visit our website:
www.lockdownpublications.com

Follow us on Instagram:
Lock Down Publications

Email Us: We want to hear from you!

In Loving Memory of
Clarence Davis

Acknowledgements

In the movies, they roll all the credits at the end. In the books, we dish them out first. So I guess it's only right I start with God. I know y'all like he writing all this gangsta ish and thanking God. Now, y'all know He done seen and heard it all. Plus, it's just fiction, a form of art. And I'm happy to have the tools to do this. Not to mention, an innovative and capable team. I got a really big team...and we doing really big things. Of course shout-out to Lock Down Publications. But right now I'm talking about these particular members of my family: Poncho, Bridget, Johnny, and Gloria. They helped me progress from behind the wall, from my own publication to this newfound partnership with the most storied publication in the business.

Shout-out to the entire LDP staff and the honcho Ca$h who got a young boss soaking up the game like a sensei. I would drop a few other names, but I'm just as excited for y'all to get to the book as y'all are to read it. This ish finna get good.

Prologue

200 sat inside a dated Acura with his roguish squad, all wearing serious faces. Hours had passed. In fact, this was the third night in a row they camped out a few houses down in this Oak Cliff neighborhood, waiting for their potential victim to arrive.

"We should probably roll, cuz," the goon in the backseat suggested, conscious of his surroundings and growing a little antsy. But 200 squinted through the murky clouds at a pair of headlights coming down the street.

"Hold on," 200 said, peeping the car's silhouette. "This might be him." Or so he hoped. The Highland Hills hardhead had been on a mission over the past year plus, preying on local dopeboyz and racking up a serious body count in the process. His brazen actions put the streets on notice, and it was all in hopes of buying a home for his mom. At least, that's what he claimed. He wanted her to raise his promising young brother in a better neighborhood.

Though most of the money that crossed his hands was usually squandered on extravagant gifts, expensive cars, clothes—mostly that high dolla shit, vacations, strip clubs and supporting his gambling habit. But this was different. This was a stash house that belonged to an underground legend, and after doing his due diligence, he learned there was over a million dollars cash inside it. Something that would surely put him over the hump. The type of trap this revered jackboy had to have.

Seeing 200 sit a mask atop his unkempt taper, the nerves in the car became palpable. You might as well have said the police were on the block.

"So, is that him?" the goon on the passenger side asked as he began to study the car too.

200 put a choppa on his lap the size of a small pole, he didn't readily answer. He continued to squint his beady eyes at the approaching car until it hit the lights and pulled to the curb slightly past the house. The occupant hopped out, but it was a female and not the dude they'd been casing the home for. "Nah, it ain't him," he said in a whisper of defeat. They were about to tuck their guns and call it a night, until another car pulled up directly behind the first. He watched as dude put his feet on the damp pavement then looked around suspiciously before proceeding to the house. He could tell that cocky strut from a mile away.

"Yo, that's that bitch ass nigga Buck right there. Mount up," 200 said. Pistols began to click and clack inside the car. While all the car's dark-dressed occupants looked to 200 as if he was their general. And when he gave his command, they masked up and jumped out.

"C'mon, it's go time…"

Chapter 1

Six Months Earlier...

On a picturesque spring evening that was sure to bring everybody out the house, 200 sat at his brother Jaylen's football practice. He had on black joggers, black Dior shoes and concealed a black Ruger under the designer shirt he wore. He wasn't on no bullshit. He just loved to wear black and didn't leave the house without the strap. Even for something as innocent as one of Jaylen's functions.

He watched from the bleachers like a proud papa as his fourteen-year-old brother did his thing. It seemed, now, that everyone wanted a piece of his brother, Jaylen. The gifted student, who planned to attend perennial power Duncanville High in the fall, drew national attention when he caught five passes for one hundred sixty-eight yards and two touchdowns at the NFL's eighth grade All-American game. When asked by reporters what his dream was, he always answered, "To play in the NFL." And with the Texas sized hype that surrounded him, it didn't take a rocket scientist to figure out the kid was destined to play on Sundays.

Feeling his phone vibrate, 200 pulled it from his pocket. He saw that it was his baby mama calling. *Oh, her ass again*, he thought. He casually slid the phone back in his pocket, then dug out a bag of sunflower seeds and opened them. He was splitting the ranch shells with his teeth when a roar rose, causing him to look up towards the field.

"Alright...show 'em how them Goodwin boyz do!" 200 yelled, watching Jaylen take a handoff then reverse field. He bounced around like a rabbit on a defender, then stiff-armed another one before sprinting forty yards to the house. "Whoo, I wish I would'a recorded that," 200 reeled with his fist to his mouth. As the team gathered up for a pep talk, a white spectator came over and complimented his brother's abilities. Then, a few minutes later, a loud whistle blew signaling they were done for the day. He began to smile unconsciously watching his handsome brother approach.

"Boy, you gon' make me come up out this shit and put that hat to you," he boasted.

"Aye...I'm hungry, Jason," Jaylen said, calling 200 by his real name. "Let's go to McDonald's?"

"It's all good," 200 patted his shoulder pad.

They began to walk towards 200's Tahoe with him teasing Jaylen about taking a shower before hopping in. Everything was cool, when suddenly he tensed up, seeing a car veer in his direction. He was about to draw down. Then he saw it was his baby mama. "Get in the truck," he told Jaylen, handing him the keys. As always, the Black and Mexican mami was lookin' good. But the way her door slammed he knew she was finna come with an attitude.

"Can we talk?" Sabrina sassed with her arms folded.

"Nah...maybe later. I'm kinda in a hurry right now."

"In a hurry for what? To slide off with one of your creepas?" Her insecurities were really starting to show.

"What is it that you want, Sabrina?"

Her voice took a softer tone.

"My six-month lease is due to come up and I wanted to see if you would go 'head and pay it."

A smug smile covered 200's face. He loved to keep her heated.

"Well, this should be a good time to start looking into somewhere cheaper. A downtown mid-rise ain't really the place for a jobless student to be staying."

"Really…" Sabrina said, squinting her pretty eyes at him. She was thinking about all the money she gave him. The money he said he was gonna give back. Six months ago, she was the beneficiary of her grandmother's insurance policy. She bought this cute lil' Camaro, paid off her remaining tuition and gave 200 one hundred fifty racks. At the time, they had been together for eighteen months. He was supposed to flip the money and make sure them and the baby were straight.

She didn't know he was gonna start actin' funny. He would tell her he was going out to hit the streets and would be back in a week. But a week turned into two and two turned into three. It was to the point where he now had his own apartment and she didn't know where they stood.

"So, you can afford to buy all these fancy cars and nice things but you can't afford to keep me in a nice place for your son?"

"Calm down. I neva said all that." Just then, a text hit 200's phone. That's when he remembered he had to be in position to pull this next play. He pulled her into him. "Look, I gotta go. Lemme drop my lil' brutha off and I'll be over there in a minute," he lied just so she would let him be.

***

After 200 stalled her out for a couple hours, Sabrina realized he wasn't coming over. The way he did shit always seemed to irritate her, so she decided to follow him just to see what he was really doing. She stayed a couple car lengths behind him, sunk into her seat, as the slight drizzle from the night sky allowed her to move under the guise of traffic. By now, she already knew that his ass was creepin'. She'd been following him and this heifer since they left his apartment. Her pink nails gripped the steering wheel tighter from the mere thought that he was spending her bread on this broad.

She felt like 200 played on her kindness long enough, and she was about to set the record straight.

As Sabrina kept her Camaro at a safe distance, Monica's "So Gone" softly echoed throughout the car. The song had put the twenty-one-year-old out there and she wondered what made 200 treat her the way he did. *Maybe it's my body*, she thought, as she glanced at her caramel-toned breasts. She always felt that her breasts and ass made her look fat and were too big for her five foot five, one hundred- and thirty-eight-pound frame. It was like she saw herself as a cool-looking chick when she really was a goddess and any nigga she was with would be fortunate to have her.

Sabrina's face showed annoyance as they descended upon the opulent Dallas skyline. That's when she knew 200 was taking her on a date and she really started to get in her feelings. *He wanna play. That's cool*, she told herself. Cause 'Brina gon' make his punk ass find somebody to play with. As she gave chase to the accelerating black Tahoe, lights from the passing buildings slid off her determined face. She couldn't wait for 200 to pull over and prance out the truck with this broad. She would finally get a chance to call him out on his shit.

Sensing the intersection she approached was about to turn red, Sabrina slid a car length back to make sure she wasn't spotted. But the dust bucket she fell behind was moving too slow, while 200 seemed poised to fly through the intersection. She hopped in the outside lane to ensure she didn't lose him, but things took a sudden turn when the light turned yellow. 200 barreled through the four-way crossing, leaving Sabrina with merely a second to decide if she would concede or pursue. An image of the way he's been playing her popped in her head. There was no way she wasn't confronting him and this bitch.

Sabrina mashed the Camaro to a distinct hum, though at the same time the approaching light flipped red. Cars had already begun to enter the crossing from other directions.

"Oh shit!" she gasped as she released the gas then slammed on the brake.

Her heart fluttered as the powerful coupe screeched to a stop right on the crossing's thick white line. The nose of her car stuck out far enough to get clipped, so she quickly backed up behind the safety of the empty crosswalk. Just then, she remembered she had her baby in the car seat. His sleeping eyes were innocent to all the toxicity around him. But she didn't like the way 200 had her trippin'. That's when she knew what she had to do.

***

"Would you guys be needing anything else?"

"No, thank you," 200 told the white waitress who gave him a friendly smile then walked off.

200 squinted at someone a few feet ahead, before turning back to his company who was really into their conversation. She was the type of girl that money usually attracted and seemed to make an impression on every man she passed in the restaurant. 200 had kept it mum to her about where they were headed. But when she saw the branding out front she was glad he chose here. This P.F. Chang's location had a touch of class and a really cool view of the chefs who prepared the food. Plus Chinese food was her favorite, 200 was really winning points.

"So do you come here often?" she asked.

"Nah, actually this my first time," he told her. "I've been meaning to check it out. Just had to find the right person to bring, you know."

A blush covered her flawless brown skin, 200 was doing and saying all the right things. The way he was playing his cards, she didn't know how this night would end. Though she did know that she was feelin' him. There was something about his street swag. He had this humble confidence that said, *"he was the wrong nigga to fuck with."*

He kinda reminded her of the rapper 21 Savage and she had always been a fiend for a real G. "Here, try this," she offered, holding up a piece of ginger chicken.

200 was staring off into space, and when he saw her expectant eyes he just said, "Mmm-hmm."

"You ain't heard a word I said, have you?"

"Nah, I'm listening," he lied with a smile while hoping she would let him get back to what he was doing.

Unbeknownst to his date, he was plotting on his next vic. And half the shit she was saying was going in one ear and out the other. He took a bite of the chicken and nodded in satisfaction just to appease her. Then when it appeared that she wasn't paying attention, he cut his eyes back at the dude, Taj, a few tables away. Taj was a tire and rim shop owner who basically used his business as a *front*. It took him a minute to get close enough to learn his actions. But just like all of his other licks, he was down to do his research. He knew how many people Taj kept around the shop and how often he visited it. Even more importantly, he knew that Taj left the shop every Thursday night with a security bag full of dope money, always at least a hunnid thou'. A bag he planned on making his. Now all he had to do was get close enough to the dread head to put this tracking app on his phone.

"Like I was saying," the date said, trying to get 200's attention back. Her body was sunk so low in the chair that all you saw was from the top of her blue dress up. Seconds later, 200 found out why as her manicured foot crept inside his black peacoat and up his thigh until she found the ample crotch of his fitted jeans. "Now that we've seen our food getting tossed in the air, maybe you could take me back to your place and see if we could do the same."

As 200 broke her enticing spell and passively glanced Taj's way, he found the lust in her eyes again before double taking then standing up.

"My bad, did I do something wrong?" she studied his tatted face.

"Nah, hell nawl. I just seen someone I know. You just stay ready," he assured her. He desperately looked towards Taj's table and he was nowhere in sight. But his date was still at the table, so he couldn't have gone far. 200 took off like a bloodhound chasing a trail, dashing by flaming grills and steaming woks. The money at stake drove his thirsty mind and he couldn't let that get away. Noticing the restroom door swinging open, he dashed in that direction before the waitress who served him blocked his path.

"You leaving already?"

He was not getting far if he didn't plan to pay.

200 feigned a smile. "Gotta use the restroom. But you can bring the bill to our table." He pivoted past her. Finally, he caught up to the door labeled restroom then pushed his way inside. Polished gray and white surfaces greeted him. And so did the sight of a slender man at a urinal with his head back in relief, Taj.

As 200 was fishing his phone out of his peacoat, the one with the spy app on it, he heard the toilet flush. Looking up, he saw Taj walking his way then frowned in disgust. *Damn, he ain't gon' even wash his hands?* he thought. Taj bypassed the sinks and pulled out his phone instead as he headed for the door. It would have made it much easier for 200 to put the app on his phone if Taj sat it on the sink. But he couldn't cry over spilled milk. Taj was on the move. Just as Taj walked past him, 200 dramatically fumbled his phone, making it slide in front of Taj's futuristic boot.

"Oh, I got you, fam." Taj picked up the phone and tried to hand it to him. But when 200 grabbed it, he clumsily fell into him.

"Oh, my bad, dog." 200 dusted him off before steadying himself. "I'm drunka than a mufucka. I knew I shoudn'a drank lean behind no liquor."

GET IT IN SLUGS | B. STALL

Taj mugged him as he walked off like he was fucked up about the mishap. But 200 was too busy pretending to be in a drunken stupor to notice. Once the door closed, 200 stood erect, shedding the act. He threw a last glance at the door to make sure the coast was clear then smiled at how he was able to bump screens with Taj's phone. He looked at his screen and saw the locator app was active. Now Taj's black ass was good as grass.

Chapter 2

Thursday Night

"Nah, baby girl...wait til later," Taj protested to the redbone he took to P.F. Chang's. For the past few days, they'd been on each other like white on rice. And Taj knew he had this important business to handle.

"What?" she said with a wicked smile on her face. She began to kiss his neck down to his chest, while her green eyes stayed focused on him. Gratification seemed to flow from each sensual kiss. His defenses didn't stand a chance. Kneeling down on his office floor, she wrestled with his pants and freed his semi-erection.

"Girl, you gon' be the death of me." Taj shook his head right before she took his tip in her mouth, and she started to go in. He relaxed on the ledge of his desk then looked down at her bobbing head. He knew he should'a left the shop to make his drop by now. But from the way she was sucking him, he really didn't give a damn. "Got damn, girl," he groaned as a slurping sound escaped her lips. She had this unique way of giving sensations. He was almost certain that she taught a class on this shit before.

"Oh, you like that?" she asked with a smirk on her pretty face. Her voice rang out all innocent but you could tell she was up to no good. She began to jerk all the excess saliva that she left along his length. It seemed seeing his flagpole standing at attention got her hot, and she went right back to goin' in. She gripped the base of his dick, and twisted it towards her lips, taking him deep in her mouth. Being the pro that she was, she recognized that she was pleasing him and all that pretty girl shit went out the window. She was getting downright nasty.

She spent what seemed like eternal ecstasy toppin' him off. Taj had had some good head before, but none like this.

"Baby, I'm finna bust," he said, putting his hand on the back of her head. "Where you want me to nut?"

The lil freak bitch blushed. "In my mouth," she hummed. Then she commenced to go into overdrive.

She started sucking him faster and doing it with no hands, making him shoot off fat droplets deep down her throat.

"Fuck," Taj groaned. It seemed the faster she sucked him, the thicker and stronger he came. She continued to suck and slurp until there wasn't a single drop left. Then when she was sure he was all done, she started to grab her things.

"Got damn girl, you got me in here all out my character," Taj said through ragged breaths. Just then he looked up and saw the clock 12:05 AM. "Shit, I'm runnin' late." He hastily fumbled with his clothes and got himself together.

Lil mama took off towards the entrance. "Bye…call me." Taj followed her through the showroom and made sure to lock up behind her.

Their rendezvous lasted longer than he expected. Now he wasn't sure if he would be able to contact his boy, Heavy. Heavy usually trailed Taj in his whip until he safely dropped off the bag. But he remembered telling him, *if you don't hear from me by eleven, I'm straight.* So he wasn't sure what to expect when he called.

Taj rested against a tricked-out Chevelle inside a Forgiato exhibit, then called up his boy. He got his answering service on the first go. After getting it a second time, he finally just gave up. "Fuck it, I'm just gon' duck off in my low-key whip and run the shit by the spot myself. It ain't the first time and won't be the last," he told himself. Then he went about securing the premises.

A few minutes and one alert head glance out back later, Taj exited the building. It seemed seedy and dark in this alleyway, but that was by design because they didn't want people seeing their illicit dealings.

Taj hit the unlock button on his Toyota Corolla and then jumped in the whip, his security bag holding over a hundred thou. It had crossed his mind to toss the money in the trunk. But he was a businessman and had receipts to back up all of his shit if the police decided to trip. And he kept that toolie and would use it. So, he wasn't worried bout no nigga. He was a lil arrogant about his. He felt like he couldn't be touched.

Taj whipped his dreads out his face then got in traffic. The way the night traffic was moving, he should slide under the radar and get to his stash house in South Garland in no time. He turned up the radio, but like always, his mind eventually got back to the money. He was scrolling his mental Rolodex tryna to see which one of his custos might need to re-up. *Didn't the lil homie from BFL cop three of 'em bout two weeks ago,* he wondered. *I should probably call him. It's about that time now. I'ma just tell 'em I'm down to my last two.*

Taj whipped out his phone as he came to an intersection and idled behind a dated Acura. He was scrolling for the lil homie's number when the roar of a motorcycle caused him to look to his left. Hmm...Yamaha, he nodded in admiration. Being a car connoisseur, he could appreciate a nice ride. But it wasn't the blue and black bike that stood out the most. It was the big booty chick holding onto its rider. Just by looking at her, in those short shorts, he got the feeling she worked that ass for a living. He shook off his lustful thoughts of how he would handle all that. Though before he could dial up the lil homie's number, the bike's rambunctious revving made his eyes dart back over.

"Man, what the..." Taj started to say, staring at the bike's rider. The rider was burning rubber, illuminating the ground with thick gray clouds of smoke. His grip was wrapped around the clutch so tight that Taj could see the veins bulging underneath the distinct tattoo on his forearm. A cynical chuckle left Taj as the rider stared at him through his colorful helmet. He didn't know if the rider was having fun or if the nigga was tryna hold his nuts on him. But quickly that thought vanished, an alarm ensued after he heard his passenger door being snatched open. It was trouble!

"Move and you make the news," 200 warned, training his pistol on Taj before he could reach for his. In that split second, Taj thought about the option of fight or flight. But fear, mixed with a little rational thinking, made him ignore both. Sure, he was a gambler and he gambled on a lot of things, but he wasn't about to take a chance. Especially with his life.

"Now, I'm only gon' ask you one time before I start dumpin' this lead… where's the muthafuckin' loot?" 200 snarled through his mask.

Just as Taj started to ramble some mumbo-jumbo, the driver's side door was yanked open and a pistol was put to the back of his dreads. Zilla's heavy unwelcomed hand began to pat down his left side where he reached inside his belt and removed a pistol.

"Look what I found," Zilla yelled through his motorcycle helmet across to 200.

"Seems like we're both finding shit," 200 replied as he tossed the clinking security bag over his shoulder.

Zilla glanced down at Taj's unsteady arms and by the time he looked up, 200 had slipped through traffic. Turning back to Taj, he quickly snatched him up by the dreads and tossed him to the ground like a ragdoll.

"Get up…get your bitch ass up," Zilla demanded, kicking him a little to help him get to his feet. "Now I want you to take off running till I tell you to stop. And if I even think you looking back, I'm domin' ya."

GET IT IN SLUGS | B. STALL

Zilla watched as Taj wafted through traffic, pulling up his pants. He knew 200 said don't shoot unless he had to. But he just couldn't help it. His trigger finger stayed itchy. F'ough!

Chapter 3

200 was sitting on the living room floor in his apartment, a place that looked like a room at the Ritz. He was high off an early morning blunt but was still on point as he separated money from last night's play. He pushed eleven racks to the side to go towards the home for his mom—he liked to call it her ten percent. A similar stack sat on the carpet to keep Sabrina off that bullshit. And another twenty-five racks sat to the side to be split amongst the crew. The rest was going to you know who.

This should keep them happy, 200 thought, more so about the crew. *I mean, they ain't have to do shit but create a distraction and I'm the one out here on the front line making everything move.*

He walked through the swanky apartment to his garage, where he hid some of his loot. It was slightly humid from the rising sun outside. But he didn't mind being down here. This is where he kept his toys. A beautiful white Aston Martin sat next to a Pan Am Ryker which he seldom broke out to ride. He knew a mufucka would try to hate, like, did he even own a house yet? But he wasn't fucked up bout what a hater thought. He spent his bread on what he wanted to.

200 moved an aluminum shelf to the side, then opened a secret compartment that he had in the ground. He was stuffing money inside it when the ring of the doorbell stirred his built-up paranoia. He paused and looked around. This kind of spoke to where his head was at. The twenty-four-

year-old was always edgy and on his toes. He quickly realized it could'a been the Twinz, who he'd been expecting. But he hurried everything back in place and whipped out that dick-knocka anyhow. With all the bullshit he stayed pullin', a nigga like him wasn't taking no chances.

200 hustled through the house to the door. But once he peeped it was his two most trusted soldiers, his whole demeanor changed. He had been cool with the Pruitt Twinz, Shocka and Zilla, since high school. They shared an affinity for football, and after practice, they would get with each other and party and bullshit. Life eventually took them their separate ways. But with them falling off into the same shit, it seemed like the thug universe brought them back together.

"What up, Zil? What up, Shock?" 200 asked, letting them inside. The two were tall like NBA guards, had bodies as stiff as the *Cliff* they represented, and wore bushy beards that fit well over their brown skin. Hell, if it wasn't for Shocka's distinct tattoos, 200 wouldn't be able to tell the two apart.

"Oh, you got it, my nigga." Zilla dapped him up warmly. While Shocka, the one he seemed to rock with harder, looked at him and rapped this Yella Beezy hook from "Headlock," his adopted anthem from the team.

"Young niggas round me roguish...you ain't gotta ask I'm totin'...Big fo-five I'm focused." You couldn't tell him that he wasn't swagged out. They shared a laugh and a handshake. Then Shocka kicked back on the couch and pulled out a blunt.

"You wanna hit this?" Shocka offered 200, once the kush aroma was in the air.

"Nah, I'm good," he declined. "I popped a few Percs and smoked one to the face before y'all came. I guess that lick had me on some celebration shit." His tatted face formed a smile.

"Well, can a nigga celebrate with you?" Zilla asked, referring to their cut.

200 lifted up the cushion of his plush suede couch then removed two large blocks of cash. One or Zilla. One for Shocka. Shocka thumbed through the money with contentment while Zilla displayed a frown, kinda like he used to back in the day when 200 used to pull all the hoes.

"What's this?" he asked. "I thought you said the lick was for over a hundred thou."

200's expression began to mirror Zilla's. "It was, nigga. That's why I threw in an extra five racks. Y'all should each have twelve-five a piece."

"Nah...nah," Zilla shook his head. "It's gon' be more like ten. We still gotta pay Tasha. She was there and ready to bust her gun like eebody else."

200 dropped his head and took a deep breath, something to quell his rising anger. He wanted to let the shit go, but in his head, it was like Zilla was tryna dictate how he run his. And that was something he couldn't go for.

"You know, for a nigga who just dry ass shootin' in the air and shit, you sholl do sound ungrateful."

"Oh, you know me," Zilla smiled. "I be ready to let that bitch ride."

"Nah. What I know is that I told you not to bust ya gun unless you had to. You could'a made shit hot for us. And to top it off, you ain't even hit shit."

Shocka began to cough up a lung then held the blunt out, his way to diffuse the situation. He knew his brother was thirsty and that 200 wasn't coming off another red cent. He was just trying to get the vibe back comfortable. "Say, this blueberry cookie shit the truth. Here, try it." He waved the blunt back and forth. His hand hung in the air for a few seconds. Then Zilla grabbed it, hit it a few times, then put the thick blunt in rotation. Minutes later, everything seemed as if it were all good. Zilla began to tell them a story about some bitch he met at Big T's Bazaar. But 200 felt like they could pop shit some other time. The nigga done already blew his high with that bullshit. Plus, he had to make a move.

"Say, I'ma go get up with the BM." He stood. They talked for a few more minutes, and then 200 showed them love and led them outside.

***

200 arrived at Sabrina's mid-rise about thirty minutes later. He was actually anxious and excited. He hadn't played house with his baby mama and his son in a minute. He parked his truck then got out next to her shiny red Camaro. The sun had risen a little more, now he was starting to regret wearing all this black.

Walking towards the first story of the modern building, 200 checked his fresh on the sly. He was rockin' a playa shirt with the skinnies, some Dior shoes that looked like J's, not to mention every piece of jewelry that he could find. A knowing smirk rose on his face. He was drippin' like a faucet and didn't think he would make it in the house good before Sabrina rushed to get a sip.

He went a little further into the complex, then entered the walkway of a door which read 8. As he found his key, he noticed the birds chirping as they flew across the manicured grounds. This is one of the reasons why Sabrina originally chose this place. It was only ten minutes from her classes and even further away from the rah-rah that plagued her hood. He stuck his silver key into the doorknob, but for some reason when he turned the key, the knob would not twist. Frowning, he pulled the key out then made sure it was the right one. When he saw that it was, he stuck the key back in and repeated the process again. Only this time he twisted it with more determination. But it still wouldn't budge. Damn, he could'a sworn this was the key.

Knock! Knock! Knock! He pounded on the door like a landlord who wanted their rent.

Sabrina heard the knocks and his familiar voice calling her name and darted for the door. She desperately wanted to open it. Lord knows she missed him. But she had to remain strong. She couldn't allow him to do this to her anymore.

"What?" she asked with her ear to the door.

"What? What you mean, what?" he countered. "My key ain't working. Open up the door."

"It ain't working, Jason, 'cause I changed the locks. I'm sick of you playing all these games. I don't have time for you or your shit no more."

A cynical laugh left 200. "Oh, so you did this shit?" He was used to Sabrina throwing tantrums when she didn't get his attention. But this time she took it too far. "Man, you trippin'. Last time I checked, this was *my* house too. You just gone up and change the locks on a nigga? When was you gon' find time to tell me?"

"Time...really, Jason. You standing there talking about time. That's funny, 'cause I ain't think you knew what that meant. I mean, you sholl didn't know the other day when you said you was coming by after you dropped off Jaylen. Or was you too busy parading around town with your broad? Why don't you go over there and spend some time with her?"

200 twisted the doorknob again. He was starting to get mad. "Look, Sabrina. Open the doe. I'm not finna be yelling back and forth with you puttin' my business all out there. My business ain't for everybody to hear."

"Why don't you just leave, Jason? You don't care about us. All you care about is your brutha and the streets. So why you even here?"

It was then that he could hear the pain cracking in her voice. She musta believed what she said. And that was far from the case.

"Dang, Sabrina. You really blowing this shit out of proportion. Sorry I ain't been coming over how I'm 'posed to. But if you would just let me in, then I can explain. Got damn, baby. I miss y'all." He put a lil' extra sauce on it. As he continued to speak, he could feel her presence at the door fade. Her energy was no longer there. She didn't even respond to the plea he was making. "Sabrina…Sabrina," he called to no avail. He stood at the door a few seconds longer before finally saying fuck it and walking off.

He was only halfway down the walkway when he realized he had the envelope full of money for her six-month lease. A lesser man would have kept going but he turned back around. Even though he played games from time to time, he still cared about her. He slid the money inside the mailbox on the door. This was the least he could do.

Chapter 4

The Next Day

Standing amongst a sea of heavy hittaz, 200 studied the action at this secret gambling shack. The house was called, "The Shack," but there was nothing shack about it. You could eat catered food, mingle with half-naked women, drink from an eclectic variety of liquor, or shoot dice until you broke up the game. But only if your money was right. Head, the homeowner and chief of security wasn't just lettin' any random ass nigga inside his seven-hundred-thousand-dollar abode. The respected goon had to know you, and most importantly, you had to be swimming in change.

Snake eyes. Damn, 200 shook his head watching some dude lose two racks out the gate. He stood on the fireplace, eyeing the multiple games and yearning to jump in the fray. But shooting dice was all about timing to him. He was gon' sit in the cut until he felt the time was right. "Hunh," he said, offering the guy next to him the loud. But the man declined and he hunched his shoulders and went back to smoking on the blueberry cookie.

There were several niggas tossin' money around as if it was nothing, which made the jackboy in him begin to plot. He made a mental note to ask Head about a few. From time to time, Head would throw a dog a bone and right now, these niggas was looking like food.

"Need a drink?" a sexy voice offered him, cutting him out of his contentious trance.

GET IT IN SLUGS | B. STALL

200 locked eyes with the girl then unconsciously licked his lips. Her beauty and body seemed to have that effect.

"Nah, I'm good," he told her, declining what she was really offering. All Head's girls sold pussy and as enticing as it was, he wasn't into trickin'. He watched the way her booty moved in her purple satin boy shorts as she walked off. Damn, he shook his head. Head sure knew how to pick 'em.

Once her spell loosened, his attention fell back to the dice games. All around him dice were clicking and fingers were popping. But one circle, in particular, seemed to be the liveliest. He slid the blunt roach inside an empty Grey Goose bottle then folded his arms and became observant of the action. There was this stocky bald head dude wearing a tank top and dress slacks, who kneeled to the floor and shot dice like he had to have it. He was up at least twenty grand and seemed to be the hot one of the bunch. All you kept hearing was his loud voice and animated cheer. *Who was he?* 200 asked himself as he watched him closer. He noticed the timepiece over his dark skin which had no stones, but he knew it cost a grip. The other hustlers had to have some type of respect or fear of him, or both. He was saying outrageous shit, talking to them like they were peons.

"Got damn, Buck," the light-skinned dude conceded. "You just too hot today. I know when to move around."

After raking dude's cash in, Buck looked around. "Next!" he called out, eyeing the select crowd. Sweat gleamed on his head from the liquor he consumed. He kept taunting the crowd as if he were Rick Flair. 200 wanted to shut him up.

"I'll fade you. What you tryna shoot?" 200 asked.

"That's what I'm talkin' 'bout, somebody with nuts."

"Bull nuts," 200 capped as he dug bands out from the waistline of his Gucci belt. He had about twenty on him right now and another twenty in the truck. He tucked his small gold chains in then kneeled down in front of Buck and said, "Shoot a rack."

"It ain't nothin' chief, shoot two," Buck countered. They both dropped the money then Buck grabbed the dice and did his animated shake. He thought he was finna hit, but as soon as he rolled, 200 stopped the dice with his shoe. Buck quickly grabbed the dice and did his animated shake again, and when he rolled, 200 stopped the dice once more. Clearly, he was tryna knock him off his square.

"Are you gon' let me roll or what?" Buck asked. "Or are you too scared to lose these lil' twos and fews?"

200 had Buck right where he wanted him. "You right. Go 'head and shoot," he raised his hands. Buck glared at 200 with an attitude. He shook the dice and rolled his point. Then, a few rolls later, he was crappin' out. This was a good start for 200. But what he didn't know was Buck really had it and what Buck could afford to lose, 200 couldn't. After an hour, 200 had to go out to the truck and get the other twenty bands.

"C'mon, hot boy." Buck waved him over once he stepped back inside past security.

Hot boy, 200 thought. You got that shit right. I outta put yo ass in the trunk and show you how hot it gets. He clenched his jaw and dug in his bag.

"Ooh...what you got in there?" Buck capped. "Fendi. Yeah, I like Fendi stuff too."

200 dropped a band on the floor. "Shoot a rack."

"A rack? Damn lil' brutha, I still gotta pay the house, not to mention my trickin' bill. Now is we gon' bet some real money or what?"

"Nigga, that's what I'm shootin'. If you don't like it, find another fader." 200 was in his feelings but he was tryna act civil. He wanted to check something. But what could he say? Buck was winning fair and square. As Buck beat him outta one band after another, 200 began to zone out. A part of his mind was thinking how he could have been at Sabrina's tryna get back right with her. He didn't think he would miss her this much. But he did. And if anything, he just wanted to spend some time with his son.

Five racks later…he was wishing he would have just given the Twinz a larger cut. They've been loyal to him and held him down to the fullest. He was all fucked up. His mind was all over the place.

"So you just gon' let me shoot? Ahhtt…where yo head at?" Buck hit his point. "Look, what you got in that mufucka?" he asked, staring at 200's Fendi bag. "Whateva it is, I wanna bet that. I'm tryna give you some action back."

200 thought about the thirty bands he'd already lost. He didn't feel like stayin' here shootin' dice till the morning with this extra ass nigga. Either he was gon' get it back or dude was gon' have to break him. He dumped his money on the floor. "That's ten right there. Bet it straight on ya point." As Buck prepared to shoot, 200 felt his lips curl to a smile and a sense of hope wash over him. He couldn't wait to watch Buck fall off his point. He was gon' get to do a little cappin' himself.

200 waited for him to finish his theatrics then caught his dice. He sent the dice back to Buck, one by one. Then when it appeared as if Buck was going to shoot, he acted as if he was gonna catch them but let the dice roll.

"Eleven!" Buck laughed obnoxiously. "I'll take that point all day."

200 grabbed his bag from off the floor, then walked off broke and feeling some type of way.

Chapter 5

Coach Phil had made it out the hood so he was no stranger to it. But the deeper he drove into Highland Hills the more his thick brows rose. The potholes. The deteriorating homes and businesses. The weeds sprouting from the paved concrete. This might have been the most decrepit part of the city. He nudged his blue Duncanville cap off his forehead as he peered out the windshield of his Ram 1500.

"You sure you're good right here?" Coach Phil asked Jaylen.

"Yeah. This my hood," Jaylen laughed. "It might look that way but it's really not that bad." After a slight pause, he added, "What? You scared?" Jaylen had built up a rapport with the assistant where they joked around. They had a bond that extended far beyond the white lines. With Renee suffering through a disability and 200 staying on the go, Coach Phil stepped in and helped however he could. He got him acquainted with the new school and gave him advice about recruiting. He even paid for his football camps on more than one occasion.

"Scared…nah, I just look square, trust me. I might know a lil thing or two about that Triple-D."

Spotting his friend, Jaylen pointed. "Can you drop me off here?"

"On the corner? I don't know, Jaylen. Maybe I should just take you home."

"Home? This is my home. My house is just a few blocks away. I'm just finna catch up with my friend to show him this article." Reluctantly, Coach Phil pulled to the curb. Once Jaylen jumped out he looked at his feet then added, "Oh, and Coach? 'Preciate the shoes." He was referring to the six-hundred-dollar Yeezy's Coach Phil bought him. They had him walking with a little extra pep in his step.

Jaylen shut the truck's door. And as he walked under the clearing skies, he looked back and noticed that Coach Phil still hadn't left. He was watching to make sure he was safe like he was one of his children. Jaylen chunked the deuce to let him know he was good and seconds later, the Hemi hummed off.

Jaylen walked with excitement in his veins as he made a beeline in Ju's direction. "Yo Ju," he called as he crossed the street but Ju didn't hear him. Jaylen peeped that he was still rocking the nappy fro, his usual block boy regalia and the way he kept his hands in his pockets suggested he was out here hustling.

"Bro, yo skinny ass ain't getting no money. I know you hear me."

Ju looked around recognizing the voice and smiled when he spotted Jaylen.

"Oh, snap. Well if it isn't Ezekiel Elliot," he complimented his football prowess. Their hands met with a crisp clap.

"What you on?" Ju asked.

"Nothing. Just seen you posted and hopped out to show you this…Bam!" Jaylen held out a magazine, drawing confusion from Ju.

"What's this?"

"It's the *Sports Illustrated Future Issue* where they highlight kids who they feel are up next. And guess who they did an article on?"

"Nah. No way," Ju said, filling in the blank.

"No cap. You can see for yourself. It's right there. Page fifty-six."

Together they turned through the pages so fast it's no wonder they didn't come loose. Ju flew by one too many pages and Jaylen backed him up.

"Right there, see."

Finding his friend's face, Ju sang with a smile, "Ayeee! Already. Jaylen Goodwin. The Lebron James of football." Jaylen was sitting in Duncanville's locker room rocking his pads and game day uniform. Peach fuzz covered his pubescent face and he looked handsome as ever.

"Dang, this is a big deal. This means you headed to the league. You gon' be livin' that boss life. Bentleys and mansions and all that."

Jaylen smiled humbly. "Yeah, that would be nice. But first I gotta get through high school. For now, I'll just concentrate on that."

As they walked by the neighborhood houses, another thought hit Ju. "Aye, when you do blow up can I have all the groupies you don't want?"

"Nah, but you can have my comb to run through that nappy head."

The pair began to laugh, but their laughter died prematurely when they heard someone hawk a loogie towards the ground. Jaylen looked ahead and saw a group of guys blocking the sidewalk. They were a tad bit older, a little taller and they all were wearing blue.

Jaylen recognized their faces but didn't know their names.

"What's up?" Jaylen asked to excuse them through. But the tall, dark-skinned one stood firm with his arms folded.

"Them shoes, that's what's up."

Another bad ass on a bike instigated, "Yeah them hoes nice. You want 'em?"

"Nah, you don't want them," a cooler head from their clique told them. "That's 200 lil brutha. That nigga right there square business."

"Yeah you better listen to ya guy," Ju suggested. "Them shoes bro got on don't come with nothing but heartache and pain."

But this was like a shot to the tall one's pride. "Man, fuck 200. Y'all talkin' all that shit like he like that. Well, where yo bitch ass brother at now?" he stepped in Jaylen's face.

***

200 stood flustered in the living room of a Poly stash house, questioning his contact's intel. For the past hour, they had been trying to get their mark to tell them where the dope was at and he kept giving the same answer. "Fuck you. I ain't telling you shit." The ése seemed maniacal and detached from what was taking place, which had 200 wondering if he was sent out here to Fort Worth on a dry run. Then as G and Shocka could be heard tirelessly dismantling the other rooms, 200 noticed a smug smile surface through the bruises on his face. *Nah, this nigga playin' games,* he thought.

Enraged, 200 took the butt of his .44 and struck him dead in the face, right on his meaty nose. Blood ran from his gash, heavy and thick. And had he not been bound to a chair his portly frame would have slid to the floor. "Pacheco…Pacheco," 200 cupped his chin. "If you don't open your eyes soon it's gon' be hell to pay." 200 was gauging to see if he could open them at all, when a masked Shocka entered the room, shaking his head.

"Yo, I ain't find shit."

Then seconds later the floor squeaked, announcing G's presence before he entered the room. He wore a mask to cover his crunchy black skin and long braids. But he stood a mammoth six-two, three hundred twenty-five pounds, and there was no hiding that. "I found something," G said excitedly, holding a trash bag in the air. G was just doing what he did best, making shit happen.

200 clapped his hands. "I knew there was some dope in there!" But after rummaging through the bag he began to feel for more.

"Nah, this ain't it. He said there would be five."

"Who said it?" Pacheco rose from his slumber in defiance. "Cause whoever it was, I want you to tell them to suck my dick!"

Fed up, 200 produced a hunting knife from his pocket. If he didn't know who he was fucking with, he was about to find out. With no hesitation, he plunged the jagged weapon deep into his thigh.

"Aahh! Oh shit! Oh my God!" He screamed horribly but 200 kept digging, letting his shrieking cries feed his anger.

"G, go find me some gasoline. I got sumthin' for this nigga. He wanna act like he don't know where the dope at. Well, let's see if know after this." As he waited for G to return, he took the knife and rotated it, making Pacheco grumble hysterically. "Nah...Nah. Don't bitch up on me now. You wanted to keep the dope and that's cool. But you won't be keeping this leg."

When G returned with some lighter fluid, 200 took the can and began to douse the wound on Pacheco's thigh. It was now or never.

"Stop! Paron! There's no más..."

"What? Don't nobody understand all that Spanish shit. If you got something to say then say it," 200 commanded.

Pacheco spoke as clear as his heavy accent would allow. "Look, there's no more dope in the house," his eyes widened. "No más. I only had fi –"

G stepped forward. "Nope, wrong answer." Two eardrum-busting shots exploded against the dead man's head, cutting his explanation short. "Let's get the fuck outta here."

200 smacked his lips. "What was that about? It sounded like he was about to tell us where the rest of the dope was at."

"Fam, you trippin'. If he ain't told us by now, then he ain't tellin' us. Let's get out this bitch while we still gotta chance."

They ran out of the tacky-colored home into the bright alley, pistols by their side. You never know what kinda traps these crazy ass Mexicans had laid. They were protective of their turf. The trio stayed on point until they got to their car.

***

200 waited for the heat to die down before he had to get up with his goons the next morning at his mom's. This is where he stashed most of the drugs from his licks. It wasn't the cleverest spot in the world but it was a spot that niggas knew not to fuck with. He hopped out the truck then headed for G's ride. He saw that the rain had cleared but the sun was still taking its sweet time to rise. And so were the hustlers it seemed, as he looked towards the corners. He thought the streets were quiet for it to be the first. Rain or no rain.

"Say, I'ma run in here and grab that for y'all," 200 told G and Shocka. Shocka responded by firing up a blunt and 200 turned and walked in the fence to go get their cut from the play. The streets were rundown in this neighborhood but the homes were modest. His mom paid rent at this brown brick, three-bedroom flat. It was nice compared to the others. And the best part was she was a ways away from the drug activity. He took his key out. Surprise. It still worked.

"T," 200 called, though his mom's name was Renee. It was a habit for a nigga around here to call his moms T-Jones, but he just called her T for short. He heard her hearty laughter and followed it to the living room. Renee had the phone glued to her ear and was watching a wild episode of *Love & Hip-Hop Miami*. Her fine hair was wrapped in a red scarf and her brown skin glowed with youth. 200 knew he would have to keep that burner close. His forty-seven-year-old mom was still a looker.

"Boy, move." Renee shooed him from in front of the TV as he tried to get her attention. She erupted in laughter shortly after she got back to her call. "Girl, nobody... just my nappy head son...dropping in." There was a thrill to her voice as she added about the show. "Here they go, girl. She tying up her hair." Binging on reality TV was Renee's unofficial pastime and like an old person watching soap operas, she hated being bothered.

"Well, dang. I love you too," 200 approached the couch for a hug. Renee playfully fended him off.

"You making me miss the best part."

200 burst out laughing. He loved getting on her nerves. She had the type of personality that brought the playfulness out of a person. "Well, where Jaylen, since you all into that show?" He feigned mad. But in his eyes, his mother could do no wrong. She was the sweetest most caring person that he knew. A motorcycle accident from her hot girl days left her with a slight disability. So she worked from home as a claims adjuster. It didn't pay much, so 200 helped out as much as he could. As Renee half-heartedly pointed down the carpeted hallway, 200 reached in his pocket and placed the eight hundred dollars for her rent on the coffee table.

"Thank you," she said gratefully, covering the phone.

200 said, "Don't mention it," then headed toward the kitchen to get the dope. He'd been hiding the paraphernalia here since his teen years because the average person wouldn't think to look past the cabinet wall. He passed Renee's Febreeze-scented bedroom. But upon hearing some activity from Jaylen's, he decided to peek in.

"Yo..." he announced himself.

Jaylen stopped working out then pulled an earbud from his ear. "Oh, what up, Jason?"

"Shit. Just heard you in here huffing and puffing," he studied him. "I see you in here gettin' it in."

"Yeah, this Moneybagg Yo got me all the way turnt."

"You fuck with that nigga?"

"Yeah, him and them Memphis boys be going hard."

200 was about to agree when he found himself squinting at Jaylen's face. "What's that?"

"What's what?"

"Mmm...that red split on yo lip. Looks like you got into a fight."

"Man, I did..."

"You did!" 200 stepped inside and closed the door as his face painted with fury. "With who?"

"Some dude named Cap."

"Crip Cap?"

"Yeah. I was just walking with my boy, Ju, showing him the article. Then dude walked up on me talkin' 'bout what's up with my shoes." Jaylen pointed at the Yeezy's.

"T bought you them?"

"Nah. Coach Phil bought 'em for me."

"Yo Coach?" 200 repeated, frowning at him in confusion. He sighed roughly from his nose. He didn't even know where to start. "Man, first of all, yo coach ain't got no business buying you no shoes. And second, you can't be hangin' out. You got too much going on for yaself. And you know how these Highland Hills niggas be."

"But I smashed dude. And Coach was–"

"But nothing, Jaylen. People know you're on your way and they want to get a piece of you. You gotta learn that not everybody has your best interest at heart. It's parasites out there," he said as he began to pace. "Fuck." This was the reason why he wanted to move his people to a better neighborhood. Just think if this simple fight would have spilled into gunplay and something was to happen to Jaylen. Now he was seeing red. He quickly blocked the thought before it had a chance to register. Then when his rage retreated, he sat on the bed next to Jaylen.

"Bro, don't think that I'm raggin' on you, or nothing like that. But I'm yo brother and I love you. And it's my job to keep you away from the bullshit. So don't make my job harder than it has to be." 200 scooted closer. "Look," he said, showing Jaylen a picture of a suburban home on his smartphone's screen. "Don't say nothing but this is the home I plan on getting for Moms."

"Wow," Jaylen took it in.

"Nice ain't it?" 200 nodded. "It's still a ways away but I'm working on it as we speak. You gotta understand that I done been out here in these streets since I was your age. And I done been through some shit that I don't ever want you to see." He reflected on some events before finding Jaylen's eyes. "Ever. You're too smart and too talented. So getting this house is just my way of ensuring you make the most of that. You feel me?"

Jaylen replied with a hoarse, "Yes." As 200 stood, he reached in his pocket and pulled out several bills.

"Here's three hundred dollars and if you need anything else, call me." 200 playfully swiped his head. "I love you."

But by the time he made it to the hallway, it was back to seeing red. It seemed smoke emanated from every step he took.

"You leaving already?" Renee tried to read him.

"Something came up," 200 said without looking back. It was the best he could come up with to keep himself from being rude. He bolted out the house, then the fence, and walked up to G's ride and patted the hood. G could tell from his expression that something wasn't right. They caught up with 200 and didn't ask any questions. They simply walked with the same purpose as the leader of their crew.

200 saw some guys posted up and approached the group of youngstas.

"Say, where that nigga Cap stay?" The first dude said he didn't know. But then he saw Jaylen's friend, Ju. And Ju told him by that tan Regal around the corner. They made it there with the quickness. And a screwless 200 knocked on the door.

Knock...Knock...Knock.

The volume of the TV seemed to go down in the house. A few seconds later, a dude who looked like a taller version of Kurupt answered the door.

"Say, where yo lil' brutha at?" 200 asked, recognizing dude's face.

"Oh, he back there in the room. Let me go grab him real quick."

A few seconds later, someone came to the door with a broken nose and a large laceration over his right eye.

"You Cap, right?" 200 asked.

"Yeah…" Before he could finish his statement, 200 drilled the seventeen-year-old in his swollen eye, knocking him off his feet. More ferocious punches came in succession.

"Yo, 200, what you doin'?" the Kurupt look-alike asked. He was about to step in but he was refrained by G's extended arm and the sight of his gun. 200 just kept crashing punches into his exposed face until he felt like it was enough.

"Nigga, the only reason why I ain't domin' yo bitch ass is 'cause you from the hood!" 200 yelled. "But let this be a lesson to you and everybody out here. Don't ever put yo hands on mine." And like that, he was out.

Chapter 6

Flashing through the night traffic in his gray Audi truck, Taj tossed a sack of kush over to Heavy. Heavy was a guy he grew up with out in Chauncey Village, one who bore a striking resemblance to Beenie Siegel but had an unnatural squint to his right eye. Taj didn't have a large team of goons like most drug dealers, but this one was sure to bust that iron. Taj continued to run down to Heavy what happened when he got robbed. He freestyled a lil bit about how he almost took the gun away. But Taj was just doing what he did best, making shit sound good.

Heavy paused from breaking down the kush. "So you mean to tell me that these niggas took six figures from you and let you live?"

It was a cardinal rule to him that you didn't give a nigga a chance to get back at you.

"Man, I'm just glad I was so quick on my feet. If it wasn't for my street instincts, I wouldn't be here today."

"Square business."

As the Audi pulled to a traffic light, a full moon glowed directly above its panoramic roof. Heavy used the light to carefully break down the last blunt. But even then the stale blunt still cracked. "Aw shit," he held the limp blunt in defeat. "We gon' need to grab more 'gars. Pull up to that Headshop across the street."

This wasn't Taj's stomping grounds, but he knew the area well. He was gonna open up his tire and rim shop in this neighborhood before a better opportunity came along.

They pulled behind a cluster of motorcycles and got out.

"Aye, I got some of that corn," a young nigga approached them.

After the fresh hustlers ignored him, he added, "I got some of dat loud too."

The two men walked in the store with Taj leading the way. It resembled the convenience store of an old gas station. And like always, there were a handful of people inside. Seeing a petite dime piece, Taj bit his lip. *Right on time*, he thought, drawn to her eyes like a moth to a flame. He proceeded down the snack-filled aisle to try to get at her. He was so caught up by the ghetto queen's essence that he lightly brushed into somebody. "My bad," he said, turning to apologize to the dude with the bushy beard. That's when he noticed dude's shiesty vibe. It was so palpable that it made a tinge of fear hit his heart. Something inside him gave him the impression that he knew the dude. But, from where?

He squinted at the tattoo on his forearm. With that, his mind began to drift. He vividly saw one of the robbers on a motorcycle as he illuminated the ground with thick clouds of smoke. He remembered how he was hitting the clutch so hard that his veins bulged under his distinct tattoo. He snapped back and looked at the tat on dude's forearm. A wave of alarm went over him.

"Aye, that's one of the niggas that robbed me right there," Taj whispered to Heavy. He'd been telling himself that he was gon' find the robbers. And here one was, walking around like shit was sweet.

"Who? Him? The one with the tats? How can you be sure?"

"That's one thing I'm good at, remembering things that are important to me. That's him. No doubt," Taj said with increasing conviction.

They watched with wicked intentions as he left the store. Then Heavy began to ease a chrome handgun from his thick waist.

***

The Twinz stood in front of their colorful motorcycles and 200's Ryker as they waited for him to come out the store. They were dressed liked badazzes, out having a good time, when it seemed Zilla's comment threw some salt in the game.

"What 200 give you for the take? Probably some bullshit," Zilla said condescendingly.

"Nah. He gave me half," Shocka told him.

"Off of five bricks?"

"Nah. It was only three." Zilla smacked his lips.

"That still ain't really shit. That nigga be playin' tight when he know he could go 'head and bless our game."

Shocka cocked his head. "Man, don't tell me you still mad because he took G instead of you."

"No," Zilla lied, when he really was pissed. "I just feel like the nigga could show a lil mo' love."

"Bro, don't worry 'bout that shit. Whateva I make off the dope, I'ma split with you. Okay?" Shocka dapped him up and everything seemed copacetic. But little did they know, it was about to go down.

***

"Oh shit," 200 mumbled, seeing Taj and his boy nod at Shocka. He recognized Taj when he first came into the store but didn't think Taj would recognize them. On the day they took over a hundred thousand from him, they all had on something to hide their faces. But seeing big boy whip that burner from his pocket, clearly they knew who Shocka was.

200 put the potato chips back on the rack then slid his Glock .40 from his pocket. It didn't matter if someone saw him with it or not. These niggas wanted to dead his boy, so it was certified murking season.

Walking with his head down, 200 stalked the pair outside to where the light pole cast an orange hue on the street. By now, both men were approaching the chattering Twinz. They were so zeroed in that they didn't even hear 200 creepin'.

Bop! Bop! Bop! Bop! Bop!

200 got a rush watching the big boy crumble and the dreadhead flip. He quickly moved in on 'em and fired more damaging slugs as one of the men struggled to get up. In the midst of his rampage, 200 heard his friend shout, "C'mon!"

He backed away from the lifeless bodies then ran and hopped on his pretty ass three-wheeler. Lights from the other bikes came to life. Then the revving of their performance bikes tore through the night.

Skwem! Skwem! Skwemm!

***

Four hours later

200 hopped out of the Tahoe and walked with purpose to Sabrina's mid-rise. It had been a long day for him so far and tonight he wasn't going for the bullshit. He surgically placed a special lock pick inside the door, then twisted the knob. It easily opened.

No one in the home seemed to notice his presence. With all this black on, he was like a burglar on the late-night creep. He went through the dimly lit home in search of his baby mama. After she cut off all contact with him, he really did miss her. He followed the soft sounds of Jaquees' version of "Trippin'" into the swanky living room. A few seconds later, a harmonizing half-naked Sabrina entered the room. She gasped and dropped her phone when she saw someone.

"Oh my God, 200! What are you doing? How did you get in here?"

200 began to step towards her as she backed up. "I broke in," he smirked. "I came all the way over here just to get this." He pulled her by her lavender chiffon robe and then kissed her passionately. Sabrina was supposed to be mad at him about something but it seemed she couldn't remember what.

When he nipped her neck, it hit her.

"Baby, stop. I said I wasn't messin' with you like this no more."

200 pressed her into the wall and flashed his knowing smile. "Who said you had a choice?" He eased his tongue into her mouth until his kisses spilled into her collar then he ripped her panties apart. Sabrina gave off a gasp of delight. She didn't know why she wasn't putting up much of a fight. But when he dropped to his knees and kissed her puffy mound, it was pretty much a wrap.

"Jason," she moaned softly. "Damn, bae…" Her sounds were rich with pleasure. It made him start to go harder. He was on a mission right now, doing things that no one else could do to her. He sipped from her well like he'd been in a desert and needed her pretty folds to quench his thirst. As her grip tightened on his unkempt hair, he knew that he was hitting all the right spots. He stopped for a second to give the small tattoo on her hip that read *200* a lil smooch. *This pussy mine*, he thought. And he meant that. No matter what they had going on or where they stood, he felt like Sabrina was gon' always be his. He slid two fingers inside her and began to suck her clit to make sure she knew. "Ooo…fuck."

"That's right, baby. Don't be keeping my pussy from me like that." Just the sight of her juicy folds had him rock hard, ready to fuck something up. He stood, then forcibly turned her to the wall. He saw that soft succulent ass and had every intention of diving in it. Though he couldn't help but toy with her first.

"Did you miss him?" he asked, guiding his flesh along her warm treasure. But he didn't give her a chance to respond. He simply kissed that spot that he knew got her hot. He slid his dick in right as she looked back and slid him her tongue. The caramel complexion goddess was all into him now. It was deeper than sex. With every stroke, she felt love.

"Mmm," Sabrina moaned as he stroked deep inside her. He was taking his time letting her make it, at first. Then he thought about how she'd been acting and started to speed up.

"Ooo...fuck, Jason. Don't pound me out. You know it's been awhile."

"You should have thought about that before you started changing locks and shit. Now I gotta make yo lil' pretty ass pay."

Sabrina placed her hand back on his tattooed stomach to try to tame his strokes. The way he was hittin' the pussy, it was like he was tryna kill it. A sexy mixture of pain and pleasure covered her face.

"You thought that shit was cute, huh?" 200 asked as he pulled her thick dark mane and put his mouth to her ear. Sabrina threw her arm back around his head and they began to kiss slowly as he grinded into her rear. He took it from the wall to the ottoman, and somehow they ended up on the kitchen floor. It was like he was taking the stress from his chaotic day out deep inside her womb. And Sabrina's parting legs would have it no other way.

"Mmm...I'm cummin," she half moaned, half-sung.

Feeling his dick throb, 200 thought about pulling out to give himself a second to recuperate. But the pussy was so good, so wet that he couldn't pull out if he wanted to. He shot off seconds later, driving his dick deeper into her hilt.

"Shit...'Brina. I swear this pussy like water." Sabrina stared in satisfaction at him with sparkling eyes. She waited for him to get off his last labored strokes. Then when he stood to his feet, she eased to her knees in front of him. She swept her hair over her shoulder then gulped the tip of his dangling flesh. Her head was slow and hot. After a few minutes, 200 was right back primed up.

"C'mon, let's go in here," Sabrina grabbed his hand as she led them to the bedroom. She felt 200 playfully smack that ass. It was time for round two.

Chapter 7

Over the next couple of days, 200 had been at Sabrina's playing house. The way they were into each other and carrying on, it was like he never left. He was relaxed on the living room couch, balancing his son on his thighs as he looked into his adorable eyes.

"Lil' Jason, tell yo mama to go make us some breakfast." The one-year-old tried to repeat what he said, which made 200 light up with laughter.

"Ugh," Sabrina rolled her eyes. "Teaching him to be disrespectful already." She grabbed him from 200. "What you want, cutie pie? You want mama to cook you some eggs and chorizo, huh? You want that?" When she saw his dimples flare, she kissed him and then gave him back to 200.

"What about me?" he teased. "You ain't asked what I want."

"Oh yeah, you," her face dropped. "You'll just eat what I cook." She was playing hardball like she was still mad about him being MIA. But she was only playing. She checked over her shoulder to see if her tight-fitting joggers had his attention before she swayed into the kitchen.

200 shook his head at the tease and went back to playing with their son. This was the break that his mind needed and he was glad he decided to duck off here. He sat his teething toddler down next to him and then grabbed the remote so they could watch some cartoons. He had begun to flip through the channels when his phone suddenly exploded

with vibrations. He grabbed it off the glass table and immediately silenced the alert. He could have put the phone away, but as soon as he found a channel, he snuck a glance at the name and opened the text. Reading the suggestive message from one of his creepas, a smile unconsciously formed on his face.

"Umm…don't you see me standing right here?" Sabrina sassed.

200 looked at her like she was crazy. "What?"

"Nigga, don't what me. I know that was one of yo lil bitches cause you sitting there grinning from ear to ear." She stormed off into the kitchen. A few seconds later, he could hear pots and pans being handled.

"Wait right here," he told lil Jason, placing him inside his playpen. He took off to the kitchen to check on Sabrina. *Fuck, here we go.* He knew he should let her be. But he had to play it off and make it seem like he wasn't doing anything. He cleared his throat as he stood in the doorway. Sabrina looked over her shoulder and immediately became more agitated.

"Jason, I'm not in the mood right now. So you could march yo ass back in there and go sit down. "

200 laughed. "Who the fuck you think you talkin' to, our son?"

"No nigga, I'm talkin' to you. Why don't you go back in there and finish textin' yo bitch." Sabrina was emotional, feeling like he was playing games again. What if he was just talking when he said he wanted to start over? The other day they talked and aired out their issues. She wanted to believe that he would be there for her and be a better father. But right off the bat, here was a sign to leave him alone. She was unconsciously mumbling her frustrations when she felt 200 ease behind her. "Don't touch me," she pushed him away. She was clearly upset. "You're just so fuckin' bold. Texting a bitch in my face."

"I wasn't textin' no bitch, bae. You overreacting."

"Overreacting, humph." She squinted at him like we gon' see. Then she pushed past him and darted into the living room, straight for his phone. When she picked it up, 200 grabbed her wrist.

"Man, if you don't put my shit down," 200 told her.

"What you want me to put it down for if you ain't got nothing to hide? Let me go."

"Sabrina, quit playin' and give me my mufuckin phone."

Her lil feisty self, managed to wrestle the phone away from him. She couldn't open the text with 200 hovering over her, so she hurled the expensive phone into the wall.

"Oh, you bet not had broke my shit," 200 warned.

"Or what? You gon' take some more of my money and buy you a new one? Nigga, fuck you. I can't stand you, Jason. You say that you love me, then you turn around and show me no respect."

They kept going back and forth. Neither would let up, until eventually, they became louder than fighting cats and dogs. 200 finally said, "Fuck it," and grabbed his phone off the ground. "You be on some bullshit, Sabrina. That's why I don't even come over here."

"Fuck you. You could leave. You ain't gotta bring yo lying ass back over here no more."

200 grabbed his things and bolted for the door. As he left the house, he heard Sabrina yell, "And I want my money too." A moment later, a hard object hit the door. *Sabrina a trip*, he thought. *And she definitely trippin' if she thinks she gon' get that money back.*

He walked to the Tahoe, then hopped inside the truck. He immediately appraised his phone and saw that Sabrina did a number on it. The case was cracked, but the screen was good. He opened the text from one of his creepas and finished reading it out of spite. There was an emoji and a few characters on the screen as he began to text back. Though his heart quickly flooded with angst when he heard someone try to snatch open his locked door.

"Get your hands up! Hands! Hands! Hands!" Different commands roared from the swarming officers. 200 looked to his left at the white boy that had his hand on the door handle. He sported a crew cut and tactical gear. There was a look of a killer in his eyes. "Don't make no moves unless I tell you," he warned. He had his gun aimed right at 200's face.

Chapter 8

200 slightly brought his head off the desk when he heard the interrogation room door open. He was downtown, at the legendary Jack Evans Building, where they taped episodes of *The First 48*. The room was cold, and even colder, due to the fact that he'd been in this position for the last six hours. The teal painted room couldn't have been no bigger than a 12 by 20, and its four walls and large two-way mirror gave you the feeling that you were already locked up. He saw the husky detective sit in front of him then put his head right back in his forearms.

"Want a square?" Detective Winters offered. When he didn't get a response, he sat back and fired one up for himself. The black man was at least fifty and had specs of gray growing on his normally bald head. Razor bumps formed underneath his chin, and when he spoke, his vibe usually disarmed you.

"It's been a long day," he said, shaking his head. "These folk got me in here following dry leads, but I still gotta do my job." He took a long drag from his Newport then blew out a cloud of smoke. "So, what got you so tired, Jason? You seem like a playa, dude. You been out here fuckin' with them hoes all day?"

200 continued not to talk, but it didn't offend him. He carried on like they'd been conversing. "Yeah, me too. I got this one chick lined up, but before I get to her, there's a few

things that I gotta get situated with you. Are you aware of what a manslaughter charge is, Jason?"

200 finally spoke. "Nah, I don't get in trouble, so this legal shit ain't really my thing."

"Well, it's when someone provokes you. It's when you feel fear, anger, or hate in the consummation of a crime against you, or someone you're trying to protect. Now, these crackers wanna slam you. But I ain't gon' let them do my people like that. I know that you were trying to protect someone when you fired shots at those two men. And it could make a helluva difference when you get to playing with these numbers. It could mean the difference between five and fifty years. But that depends on how you play ya cards."

The twenty-year vet sunk back into his chair with confidence. But the truth was, this was a mere theory about Taj and Heavy, based on bits of information they acquired. There was no surveillance footage because the store didn't have any working cameras. There were no witnesses to place 200 at the scene, and they had no physical evidence. Basically, they needed 200 to tell on himself.

200 looked up from his forearm, but this time, there was a glare in his eyes. The detective was seasoned, but so was 200, and he knew the dirty games they played.

"You know, bro, I'm a lil disappointed that you would assume that I'm this type of person. And since I ain't being charged with anything, you could consider this interview terminated."

The door quickly bolted open. Clearly, someone behind the glass was watching and listening as he conducted the interview.

"Cuff him," Detective Medlock said when he entered the room. He looked like an off-brand version of Jason Statham, and he didn't have time for the bullshit.

"Cuff him? Fuck you mean, cuff him?"

Now the detectives were the ones who weren't responding. They roughly restrained 200, put the cold cuffs on him, then led him out the door.

***

Buttons sharply clicked as 200 punched another number into the phone. For three days, he had been in Dallas County jail with no bond, and he couldn't seem to get in contact with anybody. A rough sigh left his nose as he reached Sabrina's voicemail again. He knew that she saw the police apprehend him and it fucked him up that she wasn't answering. 200 paced the dayroom listlessly as he tried to clear his head. It seemed that ever since he was brought here, he hadn't gotten much sleep.

"Yo 200, you good?" a goon he recognized from Bon-Ton asked him.

200 mourned about getting out. "Yeah, I'm straight." He dapped him up real quick, then started back pacing. It wasn't the pistol he was being charged with that troubled him. To him, that shit was beatable. The problem was that they hadn't given him a bond yet. He felt the detectives were deliberately prolonging his bond hearing until they gathered enough information to indict him for murder. He knew a paid lawyer could speed up the process and get him out.

But nobody was answering the gotdamn phone.

He decided to take a shower to shake off the filth of these county grays. After a relaxing hot shower, he headed back to his cubicle. Fortunately for him, all of his cellies were in the dayroom. So he decided to fall back on his bunk for a minute. This was that bullshit. All a nigga had to do was pick up the phone, so he could hire a lawyer to fast-forward the process. Double murder. Fuck nah. He wasn't goin' out like that. The grim prospect brought restlessness to his mind. Then when he thought about how this could affect Jaylen, he really began to brood.

200 leaned back against the wall. He knew he needed to do a better job of rejecting these negative thoughts. It was the weekend anyway. By Monday, lawyers would be back in their offices and he could hire one to push for a bond. "These hoes ain't got nothing on me," he affirmed. He took a breath and began to relax.

In a matter of minutes, he became drowsy and sleepy but still attuned to the outside noises. He managed to peel one eye open and recognize that he was nodding, but he didn't even have the energy to lie down on his bunk. He fell asleep like this though his mind didn't rest.

***

"Jason, bring yo lil narrow ass on," called Blue, 200's father as he toed quickly against the gravel in the alley. He was on a mission right now. He knew there were bails of weed inside this home and he wanted to get in it before the owner came back. He turned over his shoulder to his thirteen-year-old son, who was wearing a t-shirt with his Pee Wee football team's logo on it and a pair of shoes that looked too big for his feet. "And tie ya shoes, boy. I can't have you trippin' all over yourself." His trusted potna, Jake, wasn't too far behind. Together they were about to help the heroin junkie satisfy his morning fix.

This was the third such jux where Blue brought Jason along. He wanted to feel bad about using his son like this. But let him tell it, he wasn't in control, the drugs were. He was just doing what he had to do to get that monkey off his back.

The muscular ex-con tucked a small gold chain inside his wife beater as they approached the rear of a white two-story home. Although it was broad daylight, in a neighborhood of good homes, Blue wore no mask to hide his plaits or strong jawline. His actions were brazen. Clearly, he didn't give a damn. "Now, Jason, remember what I told you." Blue looked at his son. "The door is on the right. Soon as you get inside, I want you to immediately run to the door and let us in." Nerves began to flutter, and Blue peeped the yards and windows of the neighbors to be sure no one was watching. He saw their getaway car was up the block. Now everything was all set.

They began to hoist Jason up towards the partially open window. After he took a pocketknife and cut the screen out, his innocent face showed trepidation. "Dad...Dad," he called, trying to wiggle his way back down.

Blue fought to hold his son in place. "What...what is it?"

"I see a dog."

"A dog...don't tell me you scared of one got damn dog."

"But it's loose. And it's big."

"Yeah, but it's still a dog...they could sense fear. Don't be scared of that dog. Make that dog be scared of you."

Bullshit, Jason thought, staring into the home. The black and tan Rottweiler didn't even bark. He just growled and paced in a circle like a shark, ready to attack its prey. This terrified Jason. Why couldn't he just play football like the rest of the kids? When the men gave him a nudge, the menacing dog barked ferociously and began to gnash his teeth.

Jason pulled his head out the window. "I'm not goin' in there," he said adamantly. He began to kick his legs until they finally let him down.

"Fuck it." Blue shook his head. "I don't know how I'ma get in that itty bitty ass window, but I guess I gotta do it." He handed Jason his revolver and then appraised the window. With all the muscle he put on during his bid, it was going to be hell trying to get inside. His potna Jake was never an option. If Blue was gon' have trouble getting in there, then there was no way Jake was squeezing his big ass inside.

Slowly, Blue put his foot into Jake's palms as he boosted him towards the windowsill. He finagled one arm in but slid *down after he failed to get the other inside. "Whoo. This is gon' be tougher than I thought." Blue shook his head.*

As Blue balanced his foot so Jake could boost him back up, Jason continued to keep watch. Everything seemed to be going as planned. But then an armed man crept from the side of the house, making him give off a frightening gasp. Instinctively, he raised the '38.

Bough!

The gun went flying from Jason's hand. Blue looked from his son who was laying on the grass in shock to the large light-skinned man with a bullet in the center of his forehead. His son had saved his life but there was no time for celebration. Police sirens were rising in the distance. "Gimme the gun," he told Jake, who was closest to it. He knew if they all tried to get away, there was a good chance they'd get caught. And after robbing his son of his innocence, he wasn't about to allow him to be robbed of his freedom too.

"Y'all go 'head," he told his son and Jake. They both looked at him like he was crazy. "Go on. I'ma stay here."

200's eyes came open as the sounds of the sirens were interrupted by the C.O.'s loud call for breakfast. He looked around at his other groggy cellies, and his mind instantly went right back to getting out. It was Monday now, so he had action. He bypassed the food and headed straight to the phone to try and get in contact with his people. He wasn't about to go out like Blue, who got twenty for a murder. He grabbed the phone off the hook. He had to get up out this bitch.

Chapter 9

Sabrina sat at Dave & Busters across from PG, this guy she met a month ago.

She was wearing a tight tan dress that hugged her curves, her hair was wet like she'd just taken a shower, and her alluring eyes stayed focused on him, trying to mask the fact that she was completely distracted. Not that she wasn't into him or anything. With his business acumen and street swag, he was definitely her type. She was more or less trippin' off all this drama with 200 over the past few weeks.

It all started when she flung her phone at 200 as he was leaving after their heated argument. Her phone cracked against the door instead of his hard head. And who knew it would be a full week before she was able to get a new one and get all her numbers back. This week felt like a month for a girl who practically lived with her phone by her side. She couldn't get in contact with her babysitter. She couldn't check her social media. And the crazy thing is, she didn't even know 200 was in jail.

After their argument, the sound of her heart breaking was the only thing that filled the apartment. It wasn't until a neighbor asked her about what happened that she started to check into it. She called the police station but was given the runaround. Then by the time she was able to get through to someone sensible, he had already posted bond for some gun charge. *But why am I thinking 'bout him when I got this sexy, chocolate man sitting in front of me,* she thought. Their glances met.

"So are we drinkin? Or are you playin' the good girl role tonight?" PG asked.

Sabrina blushed. "Look at you, tryna get me drunk."

"Not drunk. Just comfortable. I don't want you thinkin' 'bout your ex... your kid...school. None of that. I just want you to take this time, have a lil fun and enjoy yaself. Is that cool?" PG looked at her with a smile she was growing fond of.

"I guess a little shot won't hurt," she said, caving in. As PG placed the order for their drinks with the waitress, she held a menu up. But most of her attention was focused on him. Being the girl that only went for thugs that she claimed to be, she dug PG's poise and posture. It made him look authoritative, like a boss. She knew this pallet recycling company that he owned was just a cover for what he was really into. Now it was time for her to peel back the layers.

"How'd you get this?" Sabrina asked, reaching past his bushy beard to a scar over his left eyelid.

"Oh, that lil scar. I got it when I was playing football coming up. It's been there forever. But all the girls think it's cute."

"Cute, huh?" Sabrina played along unconsciously, eyeing his bottom lip. Not only was he a man of great means but he was confident too. And to think, she started out ignoring his texts. Now she was starting to feel like she might have to keep him around.

Their food and drinks were brought to the table minutes later. And time seemed to fly as they continued to converse and vibe. Taking the last bite of his juicy steak, PG suggested they go over and join the crowd playing the games.

"In this dress?" Sabrina slightly protested. Smiling, PG selfishly tried to convince her why she should. Then she looked towards the entrance and saw something that completely killed her whole vibe. It was like she was seeing a ghost or something. So she squinted harder and did a double take. *Oh my God, it's 200,* she thought. His lanky brother Jaylen was not far behind. She almost whispered out of fear, but her words came off clear enough for PG to feel the urgency. "We should go," she told him.

"What's wrong?" PG studied her eyes.

His question processed slowly as she watched the brothers being seated. She feared, or rather, she *knew* 200 would take this chance to get to trippin'. But just as quickly, she felt foolish for how she'd been calling all over town worried 'bout him. Here it's been a week since he posted bond and not once has he called to check on her or their son. But he sure as hell checked on Jaylen. If it wasn't one fuckin' thing with Jaylen, it was another. *But what about me? Or your son?* she fumed inwardly. She was sick of this shit. She got one sour glance at the small snow cone on his pinky before looking off. Well, at least she knew where her money was going.

"I just wanna get away from here. That's all," she pouted.

PG didn't put up a fight which is something that won him points. She grabbed his hand and stayed on the side of his six-foot frame as they made a beeline for the door. They crossed the gaming area and a good chunk of tables. Then giving in to her temptation to look over, Sabrina saw Jaylen's eyes become electric with suspicion. Oh shit, she cursed inwardly, feeling her heart sink. But she moved closer to the side of PG's stocky frame until they were out of the restaurant and well out of sight.

Chapter 10

After playing it safe for a couple weeks, 200 was back in the mix and back on his bullshit. He sat inside the popular strip club, Diamond Carpet, sippin' from a bottle of Dom Pérignon that was merely water. Each time he took a sip, he made sure to put his sparkling new pinky ring on display. It created the facade of money while he sat in the cut, stalking his next prey.

"Want some company?" a bombshell white girl whispered over the bass in his ear.

200 politely said, "No thank you." But seeing her well-proportioned body walk away, he was starting to regret it. He would regret it even more when he found out she was a part of the select group of porn stars the club flew in. Right now, he was too busy on his own money mission. Someone had laced him up about one of the club's regular patrons who she knew kept a lot of illicit money in his home. She often went shopping with one of his girlfriends. He was here to meet her now.

As 200 scanned the lit crowd for who it could possibly be, he heard the DJ urge everybody to show the girls some love. This one guy, in particular, was doing just that. 200 began to watch him make it rain until he heard the sweet voice of the only female in his clique.

"Hey, handsome." Tasha tugged at the bottom of his white and black YSL shirt. Tasha was dark, tatted up and had this look in her brown eyes that said she stayed ready to fuck.

There was no hardness to her face. So a nigga might not know that he could be kickin' it with her one minute and end up in the trauma unit the next.

"What's up with yo thick ass?" 200 asked, gripping her luscious hips. One thing he liked about Tasha is that she stayed dolled up. Her lime green hair was cut short like Halle Berry and her nails and makeup were all on point. The black mesh shirt and panties she wore were both see through, even though it was 12:00 am and she was officially off the clock.

"You," Tasha said, checking his fresh. But then she sat on the stool next to him and her whole demeanor changed. "I got some bad news for you," she told him solemnly.

"About dude?"

"Nah, that's him over there," she said, slyly nodding to the dude he'd been watching. "He usually doesn't stay in here that long. But I guess these porn stars got him doing the most. I'm talkin' about amongst your team, within your circle. With somebody you supposed to be able to trust." She let her words marinate before she looked in his eyes and did a little probing. "Did you give G two and a half bricks after y'all last lick?"

"Two and a half?" 200 frowned. "Man fuck nah. The ése wouldn't come off nothing but three. So I gave him and Shocka a half apiece."

Just as she suspected. Tasha smacked her glossed lips. "Well, he been braggin' to my girl, putting y'all business all out there, talkin' 'bout he was one of the dudes who ran off in the ése's crib out in Poly. He told her that he hit for two and a half bricks. And he was tryna impress my girl so hard that when he took her by his crib, the fool even showed her."

With the notion of being crossed in his mind, 200 thought back to their lick on Pacheco. He remembered his contact telling him that Pacheco had five bricks and he could'a sworn that Pacheco was 'bout to tell him where the rest of the dope was right when... *The nigga G shot 'em. The bitch ass nigga*, 200 thought as his tatted face formed a scowl.

"So you sure that's what she saw?" 200 asked, holding onto hope that his trusted ally didn't up and switch sides on him.

"Yes," Tasha nodded somberly. "But don't worry 'bout that. You can get to him anytime. Right now I need you focused on him."

As they sat and watched their next vic, Tasha could see no amount of conversation could dull the fire burning in his heart. Two or three minutes went by with 200 giving her the same look. So she decided to get up and help him fix his face.

"Turn this way for me a little," Tasha told him.

"Why? What for?"

"Boy, just do it," she insisted. Regardless of what a man had going on in his world, she always had a way of easing his tension. She nudged his legs open just a hair with her knee. Then she turned around in front of him and slowly danced to the sensual sound of Jhene Aiko. "You think you could handle this?" She flirted, staring back. There was lust in her eyes and the way she swayed her hips almost became hypnotic. It seemed the way niggas stared at her, turned her on. She began to get into it, like she was moving on that D until she felt 200 pull her to his lap.

"Is he here by himself?" 200 whispered in her ear. He couldn't ignore the sexual energy between them, but he tried to stay focused.

Tasha was still mesmerized by the size of his dick. The two had never fucked and now she was starting to regret that they hadn't.

"Oh no," she stammered. "He's here with two other dudes. But he drove by himself—"

"—And you sure he keeps a safe in his home?"

Tasha reached back and cupped his face. "Of course, daddy. You know I'ma always stay on top of things when it comes to you." The rest of the song played before she stopped dancing and stood up. She sat back on the stool and ordered herself a drink. They were in the middle of a real conversation about themselves when 200 suddenly took the conversation left.

"Get the fuck out my face with that dumb shit," 200 stood. Seeing the expression she gave him, he softly explained. "The young boy. He's getting up to leave." She didn't have to look over her shoulder to know what he meant. She began to put on too. Their act was in motion.

"Baby, don't leave. It was nothing. I can explain," said Tasha.

200 stormed towards the exit with Tasha in chase.

"Bitch, quit following me," he told her.

She grabbed his hand. "I'm tellin' you, it meant nothing," she pleaded.

Their argument spilled outside into the parking lot where she explained to the security that she was okay. 200 tried to keep up with the dude.

Tasha scurried in her heels trying to keep up with 200.

"Baby wait," Tasha pouted once 200 was at dude's car. She backed him up a few feet away. And they began to whisper to each other as if they were making up.

"Can you see it?" Tasha asked.

200 started at the license plate on the rear of the car. "It says Texas—"

"Texas," she repeated.

"N0 621."

Once they both seemed to have it memorized, 200 let Tasha give him a kiss. He couldn't wait to do a Google search on the license plate because by the time dude made it home, his goons would be at his crib.

***

The Twinz had been in the house with dude for an hour when 200 pulled up. The house appeared to be just like every other house on the block, the lights were out and the perimeter was quiet. But when 200 stepped inside, there were obvious signs of a struggle.

"Aye, where y'all at?" 200 called, his voice marred slightly by the ski mask he wore.

"We back here," one of the Twinz yelled, causing him to follow the voice that led to the room down the hall. Stepping inside, he saw the Twinz masked up and standing over dude he was watching at the strip club. The fair-skinned gangsta was zip tied with his hands behind his back. He had this look in his eyes like he wasn't coming off shit.

"Did he tell y'all what the code was?" 200 asked, referring to the safe.

"Nah," Zilla seemed to take offense. "But he was about to. We got it."

200 knew this was Zilla because he was always trying to dictate something. Zilla shifted his glare back to dude and momentarily his lips parted to issue another dry ass threat. But then he saw 200 whip his chrome .38 from his side.

"I'm telling you, we got it, bro," he reiterated.

But it was too late. 200 didn't have any understanding.

Bough! A shot ripped through dude's arm.

"Got damn, bro. I told you we had it," Zilla pouted. But there was nothing more he could say, 200 had already taken over. He began to pace and pout like he was really fucked up about the situation. But he couldn't stay pouting for long. 200 was getting results.

"Now you got three seconds to tell me what the code is," 200 warned, aiming the pistol at dude's chest. He didn't give the hyperventilating man any time to plead. He just taunted him by counting down in an accelerated tone as if he planned to shoot.

"Okay…alright!"

"Okay…alright, what? I can't press that okay shit into the safe."

"It's 23…53…22. You gotta wait a minute for the security bars to slide back."

200 followed his instructions to a T. A few seconds later, he pulled the safe's handle and the door opened. "Wah-lah fellas," he said, glancing back at the gang. He pulled a trash bag from his hoodie and swept all the money inside. They all stormed out the house and left dude to fend with his wound.

Chapter 11

Detective Winters walked into his office at the Jack Evans Building, followed closely by the filming crew for *The First 48*. He was clearly frustrated from a disappointing day at the courthouse. He sat his files on the desk then his big frame dragged the chair to a screech. After staring off in space as the cameras seemed to eat it all up, he reached in his dark slacks and grabbed a pack of Newports and fired one up.

His drag wasn't meant to be dramatic like he was doing it for the cameras. He just needed a deeper pull to rid his mind of all the bullshit. He felt that with the evidence they presented, the tip placing 200 on the scene of the murders and the danger that he posed to the community, the judge should have immediately sided with them and revoked his bond. That way they could have held him behind bars where they could do what they do, apply pressure.

But 200 had a fine team of lawyers that made him out to be this saint. Clearly, Detective Winters knew he wasn't. To him, 200 was a nuisance. A problem. A killer. Now he felt a responsibility to the community to find some real evidence to prove it. Detective Winters saw the producer urging him to give some insight, so he sat up straight and cleared his throat. "It's been two weeks now," he said, speaking into the lens as if he was talking to a trusted friend.

"You know we normally love to get our suspect within *The First 48*. But sometimes...well sometimes, shit don't go as planned." He shook his head then after one final pull he put out the cigarette and brought the chair to a screech again as he stood. "People haven't been just coming forward willingly and volunteering information about the murders. But I'm finding out more and more about the man they call 200." He pulled a large mugshot from one of his brown files then faced it towards the camera. Just the look of arrogance on 200's hardened face made contempt cover his. It even spilled out in his tone.

"They're saying he's the real deal. My informants call him a jackboy who bars none. He specializes in targeting high level suppliers. And from the fear in their voices, I don't know why I hadn't heard of him sooner."

Detective Winters began to pace in deep thought. He was supposed to be at lunch. But it was hard for the diligent public servant to break when he felt he was staring into the eyes of his man. Suddenly, a thought hit him. He ran and grabbed the phone. "Yes, I want you to find out who that apartment 8 in the Regal Courts belongs to," he told the office secretary. He didn't have to wait long. The secretary had come back quickly with the information.

"Yes...okay, thank you," he said. He moved rapidly, grabbing his files, then his jacket from the chair. He looked at the camera with excitement in his eyes, "We got a lead, guys. C'mon, let's go."

***

Sabrina's pretty face grimaced as the tattoo artist took the needle over her hip. She was covering 200's name with a colorful butterfly, hoping to erase the memory of her triflin' ass ex. But the pain the needle caused was just like the pain 200 caused her in their relationship. Sure, they had some fun times together, but lately she'd become accustomed to the bad instead of the good. It was clear that he didn't value anything that was important to her. She was just trying to do all she could to help heal some of her wounds.

"It's coming out good," the artist said, wiping the ink that ran down her curvy hip with an extra dose of care and concern. Most men would look at her and think she's cute. But it was clear from her appearance that the brown skinned broad thought of herself as a dude. She wore her hair shaved on one side with highlighted dreads swooped to the other. She had piercings everywhere. And it was obvious from the lust in her eyes, she liked what she saw.

"It *is* comin' out good," Sabrina agreed. She noticed the way the artist was looking at her, and even though she didn't swing that way, there was something in her vibe that made her comfortable talking to her. "I don't know why I got his name on me in the first place."

"You was just in love, girl, that's all," the artist comforted over the reverberating hum of the needle. "But you don't need him. You're beautiful. And with a body like yours, you'll get over that nigga in no time."

Sabrina wished it would be that easy but it seemed the more she thought about him, the harder it became for her wound to heal. Close to two years had passed and 200 was like a different person from the man she used to know. She never would'a thought that he would break her heart or be a part-time father to their son. And the way he played her out of her money made her feel as if she was some nigga on the streets. She wanted to forgive. But a part of her wanted to get back at him for all that shit that he's done. She tried not to think about 200 so much, 'cause when she did all it did was rule her emotions.

"I really like the colors you added," Sabrina said, shifting the conversation back to her work.

"Stand up and look at it in the mirror," the artist suggested.

But what she really wanted to do was get a glimpse of how that ass hung in them pretty ass panties. As Sabrina stood in the wall length mirror, looking like a swimsuit model or a bad ass baddie, the artist shook her head thinking, *what a fool. If I had a bitch who was bad like this, I wouldn't lose her to no man.*

"You know, this one's on me," she said, referring to the two-hundred-dollar session for the tattoo. She passed her a business card then looked in her eyes and shot her shot. "Just when you think about getting some more work done or need somebody to kick it with, give me a ring."

Sabrina graciously thanked her, got dressed, then went outside to her car. As she stood at the door, she looked around the sun-drenched shopping complex for somewhere to eat. She was debating whether to go to this really good burrito joint or Subway when the screeching of car tires brought a tremble to her heart.

"Oh, fuck. What's this?" she gasped in panic. Two unmarked cars swooped in behind her and completely blocked her in.

"Sabrina Edwards," Detective Winters called, hopping out of the driver's seat of his Ford Taurus. He wore his gleaming detective badge proudly like a piece of jewelry. And from the frightened look on her face, he couldn't wait to start asking questions. "I'm Detective Winters and this is Detective Medlock. We're both from the homicide division here in Dallas County."

"Now we have a few questions for you," Detective Medlock added, putting on his tag team act. "Like what time did 200 get over to your house the day we arrested him?"

"I don't know," Sabrina pouted. "I was sleep." She was nervous as shit but still conscious enough to know that she shouldn't have told them that much.

"What about—"

"Look," she interrupted. "If I'm not under arrest, all I want to do is leave."

This was much to the disappointment of Detective Winters. The girl knew her rights. He thought he had himself a duck.

"Do I need to call my lawyer?" She got stiff on 'em.

"Don't worry, sweetheart. That won't be necessary. We're just trying to help admonish you of any wrongdoing for the murders before shit hits the fan." Detective Winters held a card up then placed it on the trunk of her Camaro. "If you need us." His displeasure was hidden with a smile as he and the other detective hopped in their cars and drove off.

Sabrina was still reeling even after they left. Murders. She leaned against the door of her car. "What the hell has 200 been doing?"

Chapter 12

"Damn, boy. You did your thing tonight," Head buttered up a grinning 200 as they playfully dabbed elbows in a hallway at The Shack. 200 stopped then fished out eight bands from his Fendi bag, Head's cut. With his take from the lick and his winning shooting dice, the boy had made close to ninety g's this week.

"Gotta quit while you ahead," 200 admitted. "I ain't goin' out like I did the other day with Buck." They capped for a few minutes about his winnings before taking their celebration back into Head's office. This was a spacious room which was equal to an office at a club. Surveillance monitors showed every angle of this lavish abode, and it was comfortable enough to conduct a boardroom deal. Head really had a taste for the life.

Before they could get seated good, one of Head's girls checked in ready and willing to do whateva he said. "You need anything?" she asked, her hazel, green eyes focused only on him.

"Sure, Nessa. Pour me a shot of 'gac. You good, 200?"

"Yeah, homie. I'm straight. It's too late for me to be drinkin'. I'ma just fire up this shit right here." 200 held up a perfectly rolled blunt. "This that blueberry cookie. I swear I think I'm addicted." As pungent smoke swirled around him, he watched the scantily clad woman leave the room. The snow bunny was slim-thick with a face that a nigga would wife. She seemed too good to be selling pussy, but who was he to judge.

After a few loud coughs and a few pats on the chest, 200 squinted at the surveillance monitor. "Aye, Head. Ain't that ya boy?" The center monitor showed an image of Buck coming through in his familiar tank top. He was greeting his people as if he were a politician. And from the way his lips parted, it was like 200 could hear his loud voice.

"He ight. But I wouldn't just say he my boy."

"Well, feed 'em to the wolves, sheit."

Contemplating the very idea, Head's laugh came off like a balk.

"Nah, I definitely ain't gettin' involved with that."

"What's up with dude? Why you say it like that?"

"Trouble—that's what's up. Them Golliday Boyz run a tight ship. Been doing so for years and gon' get out there on a nigga at any instant."

"But being certified ain't neva stopped no nigga from catchin' a slug. You know ups gon' always be the draw?" 200 reasoned, steady schemin'.

Head slightly sighed as he shook his head. He was thinking about the danger involved. Clearly he didn't want no parts.

"Yeah, but I fucks with you and you know that if it was sweet, I'da been put you on it. But these niggas ain't really the type to be fucked with. They fo' real 'bout that hustlin' shit and everything that come with it. I'm talking hittas and hustlaz in every corner of the city. And any mess they leave, the police come right through and clean it all up. Now what you need to do is link up with these niggas."

200 looked at the seriousness in Head's face and a laugh hummed through his chest. *Link up with these niggas? Who the fuck do I look like?* He couldn't stand Buck and wanted to see a bitch nigga like him suffer. He was even a little surprised that a goon like Head had this scary ass attitude.

"I'ma sleep on it, my nigga," 200 lied, dapping him up before he left.

He happened to walk right past the nigga Buck as he made his way out. Just the sight of the smug smirk that he gave him made his insides boil. *Fine*, 200 thought. He recognized that Head didn't want in. But the levels he revealed to Buck's operation made him want him all the more. When he got outside, he hopped in the Astin' with one thing on his mind—gettin' at Buck.

Chapter 13

A Week Later
200 had already learned bits and pieces of information about Buck. What he sold and what kind of change he was playing with. Still nothing concrete. So he shelved his hoodie and ski mask and went by his moms to get at Jaylen on the Madden.

"Here we go with all these audibles and shit," 200 teased him, as he kicked back on the loveseat next to his brother in the dark living room. It was one in the morning and they'd been at each other for hours. Their series was now tied at two apiece.

Jaylen was putting one of his defensive players in at wide receiver. "Calm down, playboy. Just hold your horses." The defensive player was a created version of himself. He was already seeing himself as a future Cowboy. "Alright. I'm ready. But is you?" he asked, switching back to the main screen.

The sound of the artificial crowd filled the living room and at the word "break," their respective teams lined up in the trenches. The score was tied with only minutes left so shit was getting real crucial. Jaylen faked a few snaps then finally hiked the ball. His created player appeared open and he threw a bomb in his direction.

"Mmm," 200 said, trying to jump the route. He thought he had himself a pick. But the forty-yard throw landed right in the receiver's hands.

"Ooh," Jaylen said before being taken down. He stood up and started hittin' the Nae-Nae on 'em. He looked over at 200's wrist. "This for the watch, right?"

"Nah, this for them expensive ass shoes that yo coach be gettin' you. Don't start celebrating too soon. This shit ain't over wit yet."

Both brothers' attention became glued to the curved high pixel plasma TV. 200 had just called timeout. It was 1:58 on the clock. Jaylen lined up in a formation that was familiar to 200. But instead of blitzing through the line like he'd been doing, he followed his instinct and started cheating in the direction he thought the pass was going. As the line collapsed around Dak, Jaylen just hurled the ball like a hustla does his pack when he sees the police coming. The wobbly ball was snagged out of the air by the defender.

"Interception!" 200 yelled. "Let me get that," he continued to cap as the linebacker made his way to the endzone uncontested. "New leader."

"Man, you ain't did nothin'."

"New leader, I say." 200 pointed at the score. They were so into the game that they forgot their mom was asleep. 200 felt apologetic when he saw her. Her sweet face had grogginess written all over it. "Oh, I'm sorry, T. Did we wake you?"

Renee adjusted her comfortable house robe over her shoulder. "No, not really. I had to get up and get some pain pills for this dang-on nerve of mine anyway. But I'm assumin' since it's so loud in here that you didn't bring my grandson. When am I going to see my chubby munchkin? It seems like it's been forever."

200 hunched his shoulders then groaned as if he didn't know.

"Oh, Lord. Y'all must be over there fighting again. What you done to that girl, Sabrina, now?" Renee always took her side. It seemed the mere mention of Sabrina's name deadened his whole vibe.

Renee noticed his salty look. She looked over his shoulder. "That bad?"

"Nah. I'd just rather not talk about it."

"Well, you need to talk to her and get this co-parenting thing down pat. 'Cause I want to see my grandson," Renee said, leaving the room. Her voice was sassy and sincere. She didn't want any excuses. She just wanted to see her baby.

As the fellas got back to playing the game, Renee's comment had 200 thinking about his son too. Even when he tried to be a bigger man and look past that shit from the county, Sabrina still wouldn't answer the phone. He guessed she was still on her bullshit. Out of nowhere, a text brought his phone to life. A text from Tasha. He put the game on pause and eagerly read it.

My girl said he out there in the houses round AMP

200 knew Tasha was talking 'bout G. He could already see himself lighting this bitch nigga up with slugs. "Here," he said, tossing the joystick in Jaylen's lap. "You got this game. I gotta run."

"What? You got a chick to get up with?"

200 looked at the innocence in his brother's eyes. "Sumthin' like that." He told Jaylen he loved him, got up and went to the door. Looks like he was gonna need that hoodie and ski-mask after all.

***

"I came to bring the pain hardcore to ya brain. Let's go inside and dash the flames." The lyrics from the car's speakers seeped so far into 200's soul that he felt like Pac when he was recording it. Ready to tear shit up.

He drove a duck-off down the street Tasha told him G would be on. Rain came to a healthy drizzle, helping him do so inconspicuously. Not that it would matter. The lone soldier was mad enough to air G out in front of a hundred niggas if he had to. He saw a few clucks and he knew he was headed to the vicinity of the red car Tasha described to him. G's fat ass was said to be out here clockin' all the sales. With all of his muthafuckin' dope.

Leaning further back in his seat, 200 squinted about the neighborhood. He saw a few nice homes, some people gathered underneath a tree and a woman that seemed as if she may blow in the wind. Definitely a cluck. He kept looking and saw some nigga in a foggy car but it wasn't the color of the car Tasha described. After dry riding in circles for a few more minutes, he smacked his lips, prepared to call it a night. For all he knew, he could'a been on a lulu mission. But something kept telling him to go back and look at the car.

200 circled the block again, only this time he came the opposite direction. He pulled a Ruger from his hoodie and put it atop his dark jeans just in case this was G who peeped him and got to dumpin'. A natural nervousness filled his heart. It was war time. He began to creep the block slowly. Even slower when he noticed the maroon-ish rental car with its interior lights on. He saw a large figure inside leaning over to serve a cluck. *Could this have been the car that Tasha was talking 'bout?* As he veered closer, he peeped someone on the passenger side. But there was something about the driver that stuck out to him. Maybe it was his dark skin, long braids, or those animated mannerisms. The driver turned just a little...*oh shit! That's him.*

He drove normally until he was out of sight, then he gassed up the car, made a right and whipped to the curb. He cracked the door, then checked his surroundings before hopping out. Nothing seemed out of the ordinary and the only sound that could be heard was the insects of the night. Hopping out of the car, he pulled the hoodie over his tatted face. He didn't bother with the ski. He kinda wanted the snake nigga to see him right before he filled him with lead.

He walked around the corner and was at the far end of the block. Now he could see a few people parlaying under the tree. One was even singing, "We're gonna have a funky good time."

Damn sho' is, he thought. He sped walked with his head down. Then as he began to approach G's car, he ran down on it and burst into action.

Over the blast of the gun, you could hear the engine revving as the frightened driver tried to gun the car and get away. But there was only one problem—he was still in park.

"F'ough! F'ough! F'ough! F'ough!

Suddenly the revving stopped and G's dead body slumped on the horn. 200 spun back towards the direction of his car and took off, feeling vindicated. Spurred by a wild excitement. Seconds later, his tatted hand reached the door. He'd left it unlocked. Then he hurriedly slid inside, grabbed his keys off the floor mat, then mashed off without turning his headlights on.

Chapter 14

Sabrina opened the door to PG's truck, then allowed him to guide her onto the parking lot of her mid-rise. She was both glowing and smiling on a late summer night as she reeled about their dinner at the famous Ball at Reunion Tower.

"Did you have a good time?" PG asked. He seemed like the perfect gentleman. But thoughts of being with her ran wild in his mind. Sabrina was lookin' too damn good, like a sexy Instagram model. Her flattened hair fell to a flirty white shirt where her caramel-toned cleavage caught your attention. And there was something about those jeans and those heels that seemed to do something to him. Bangin' as her body was, he wouldn't even know where to start.

"Actually, I did. It was nice," Sabrina admitted. "I never knew there was a restaurant inside it. I always thought that Ball was for show." It surprised her that over this last month they had been kickin' it and vibing and PG had never tried anything. He seemed content with just getting to know her. That made her want him all the more.

As she led him towards her apartment, they both seemed deep in their own thoughts. There was great anticipation in the air. This would be the first time they were alone. Her keys jingled as she pulled them from her purse and then searched for the one that opened the door. She was about to mention that she couldn't really believe the opulent restaurant rotated. Then she felt PG ease up behind her and she completely lost her train of thought. "Mmm, what you doin'?" she asked. But she already knew the way his bulge pressed into her. The way his lips found her collar. The way he seemed in control of her body. The nigga was taking charge.

Sabrina's eyes drifted to the stars in the sky as pleasure engulfed her body. This felt new and exciting. She couldn't even balance the key good, so PG guided her hand and helped them enter the house. As he backed her into a wall, she spun towards him, then tugged on his Cirόc-flavored lip and kissed him back. She swore PG could read her mind by the way their energy seemed so in sync. They kissed for a full minute before they finally broke apart.

PG looked into her eyes with that charming smile of his. "Damn, your lips taste good." He looked at her zipper. "But I wanna see how your other lips taste."

"Boy..." Sabrina said, watching him go to his knees. But she didn't have time to protest. PG had already unzipped her pants. She bit her lip, then closed her eyes and became lost in the pleasure. By the time she reopened them, she was laid on the couch with PG feasting on her. Everything from her waist down had been thrown to the floor.

"Damn..." PG groaned, coming up for air.

"What?"

He was enraptured by her puffy mound. "These lips taste better than the other ones." He buried his face back in it and began to go to work, motivated by the sweet sounds she was making. It was like she was in the studio hittin' high notes and his tongue was tellin' her just how to do it. He began to stroke her clit, rubbing it with his thumb.

"Mmm—P...G, you gettin' this pussy so wet." She rested her French tips in his waves and guided his bushy beard deep inside her nectar. Her sounds rose to a feverish high pitch. But the delight on her face was interrupted by the intrusive ringing of her phone. Her brows furrowed slightly. She knew it was 200 calling because the ringtone for Trey Songz'

"Can't Be Friends," played. They had only talked twice over the last month, and each time they did, the conversation ended in an argument. She was tired of begging him for money that was hers and to be a father to their son. She didn't want no more dealings with him. For all she cared, he could kiss her ass.

Sabrina tossed her phone to the carpet, and just as quickly, PG flipped her on her side and began to eat the pussy like that. She grabbed the couch as if it were a wall. "Mmm...shit." PG had her water balloon soft ass open, lapping from her clit to her lips, accidentally hitting her ass. Or maybe it wasn't an accident? He left her pussy and began to concentrate solely on her ass until she pushed his head back. "Okay. That's enough."

PG laughed. "Got yo ass runnin'. What, you ain't ready?"

"Nah, I ain't ready for all that." She turned on her back. "But you can put sexy lips of yours right here," she pointed at her pretty pussy.

PG happily obliged and tongue kissed that monkey as if it had a heart. His head was far superior than any man she'd ever been with. It must'a been that extra twelve years of experience. As PG stood, his dick bumped her ass. *Oh, is that all him,* she wondered. She found out seconds later after he stepped out of his Versace slacks.

"I think he wants you more than I do," PG teased, mesmerizing her with steady strokes of his length. It seemed so full and so thick. Sabrina just studied him as he took it and tapped the fine stubble around her kitty before spreading her legs wider and gently pushing in.

"Mmm," she moaned. *Oh fuck, a condom.* But it was already too late and too good. PG's stroke game was definitely official. It seemed his only objective was to give her pleasure. But after a few good minutes of rockin' the boat, he really started to dive in it.

"Aahhh…" she pressed her eyes closed. "Fuck!" She put her hands on his abs to brace him, but PG kept tryna knock it out. "Oooh, you goin' deep," she sung. "Too deep."

"Open your eyes." PG told her. "I want you to see how wet this dick making you."

Bringing her alluring eyes to his soaked muscle made the Black and Mexican beauty unconsciously bite her lip. PG just kept hittin' it…and drillin' it…and fillin' it for what seemed like an eternity. Minutes later, she was leaking all over the expensive couch.

"Oh, P—G! PG. I'm cummin'—fuck!" she screamed. Surely she would have to do some scrubbing before the night was done.

PG heard the gushy sounds her body made and anticipated that he was about to bust next. Then it seemed as if something magical happened and the buildup in his loins subsided. He noticed he could look at the way he entered her with no fear. Kinda like he popped some blue pills or was doped up or something. He smacked her flesh with each punishing stroke. The kid was in rare form.

Pat…Pat…Pat…Pat.

"Get up. Let's go over here," PG told her, envisioning her in a new position. When she got off the couch, he led her to the soft carpet, and put her on all fours. Unbeknownst to him, this was Sabrina's favorite position. With her succulent ass tooted high, she looked over her shoulder with the most wanton look he'd ever seen. It was like she knew she had that work. Knew her pussy was a treasure. She opened her left cheek, and her eyes fell to it.

"Put it in," she purred. Her invitation was as enticing to him as a red flag to a bull. PG grabbed her cheek himself then slid his full length all the way to the back of her walls.

"Aah…" she moaned in ecstasy. "Baby…"

"Oh, I'm your baby now?"

"You gon' be if you keep hittin' it like that."

PG pushed as deep inside her stomach as he could, tryna make her his. But there was only one problem, she still had strings to her old bae. Loudly and intrusively, Trey Songz', "Can't Be Friends," played from her phone again. It was a reminder of 200.

"Look what this girl done did to me…"
"…she done cut me off from a good, good love."

PG peeped 200's name on the screen and wanted to see how much she despised him.

"Answer it," he dared.

But Sabrina was too busy concentrating on her next nut to care.

"Answer it," he dared again.

Sabrina looked at the screen and actually entertained doing it.

***

200 pulled in the parking lot of Sabrina's mid-rise. He would've parked next to her 'Maro, but there was this Ram truck there that he'd never seen before. He was frowning, but not mad. More so upset. He knew she saw him calling but was still on some ignoring-your-call shit. *Well, I guess she's ready for a surprise again*, he thought, glancing in the console at his special lock pick. It had been close to a month since he'd seen his son. And if Sabrina thought she was gon' keep him from seeing him, she had another thing coming.

Finding an open space a few spots down, he whipped his big body Tahoe inside of it. He seemed oblivious to the fact that he was taking up two spaces. He was drunk as fuck, spring break drunk at that. Fuckin' with the Twinz at their private birthday party, he let loose and turned up with the guys. He saw there was a little corner left in his Rémy bottle, downed it, hopped out, and proceeded towards the house.

As 200 slowly paced towards the crib, the mild breeze brought him to little by little. It felt awkward just being around here. The last time he was, he was taken in for questioning in a double homicide. Maybe this was his conscience telling him that he was in the wrong place. Still, he reached past the pistol in his pocket and grabbed the special lock pick he slid inside it. He tried to slide it up the sleeve of his designer shirt, but it slipped from his grasp and clinked on the ground. Fruitlessly, he looked around before finding the shiny object at his feet.

"Man, I'm out here trippin'," he voiced inwardly as he snatched it up, hoping no one saw his mischief. But looking to his left, he noticed someone peeking out the window. The woman made it apparent she saw him, which brought about a sense of guilt to him.

In his heart, 200 knew he was out of pocket. These nosy neighbors wouldn't hesitate to call the police and here he was sneaking around in all black. Something kept telling him to shake the spot. But his legs had a mind of their own as he continued towards apartment 8.

The swanky apartment looked dark, but it was too early for her to be asleep. He wondered, *Would she be mad that I showed up? Would she put up a fight or would she let me see my son?* Anxiety building, he slid the special lock pick back in his palm. But when he looked over his shoulder and saw the woman standing in the door with a phone to her ear, it seemed as if she was calling the police on him. He took a few more lethargic steps before he finally said, "Fuck it," and walked back to the truck.

"Sabrina be on that bullshit," was all he could say as he started the Tahoe. "She needs to grow the fuck up. We have a son together. This shit can't keep going on like this."

Chapter 15

Drills were intensifying at the Nike 7-on-7 camp on the state-of-the-art field at the University of Texas. Nearly 200 prospects participated in an assortment of drills, while several coaches and scouts watched on and took notes as they happily endured the sweltering August heat. The prestigious event was in full swing. But the bulk of the attention seemed focused on Jaylen. He was sitting at the podium with Coach Phil, flanked by a bevy of cameras and reporters. When Coach Phil handed him a pen, he said, "I can't believe this is happening."

"Believe it, it's your moment," Coach Phil said, his words coming off with the positive assurance of a parent.

Jaylen took the letter of intent and seemed to get lost in thought. Here it was, all the hard work and effort paying out in the form of a full scholarship to one of the wealthiest schools in all of America—all before he even stepped foot into a single high school classroom. It was a relief to get this out of the way. But he wondered how 200 would feel to learn that it was Coach Phil who steered him in this direction. *Who is Coach Phil to guide you on a decision like this? I thought I told you to be wary about people who are not out for your best interest.* Well, on second thought, maybe he didn't have to tell 200 that part. Besides, at the end of the day, it was his decision to make.

Coach Phil leaned over and whispered something in Jaylen's ear. Jaylen laughed it off and signed the letter of intent. Light applause followed.

"So Jaylen, how does it feel to be a Longhorn?" a reporter asked.

"What made you choose UT?" chimed another one.

Jaylen was a natural in front of the cameras. "Well, I'm a Texas boy through and through, and UT offers some top-tier educational programs…a stunning campus. And by staying close, my family won't have to travel far to see me play."

This was important for him because with his mother suffering from a slight disability, he didn't want to inconvenience her in any way.

"Congratulations again," said his trusted mentor, Coach Phil. He left Jaylen to talk with the reporters. As he got up, he nodded towards the Texas staff to congratulate them. Then spotting one of their handlers on the far end of the field he took off to go meet him. The handler was a frail man with freckled skin and auburn hair. He wore cheap shades and displayed a smile as Coach Phil approached.

"Thanks again," the handler told him.

"Don't thank me. Pay me," Coach Phil countered in reference to delivering Jaylen.

"Don't worry. There will be a hundred thousand in your account by the end of day, as promised. And when he officially enrolls after graduation, we'll give you another hundred thousand then."

The news brought great relief to Coach Phil. Once he started to relax, he told the handler how difficult it was to get Jaylen to trust him.

Chapter 16

There was a big storm moving across the country, but the sun in North Texas seemed to have its own agenda. And like many of the partygoers at the annual DUB car show, 200 and the squad took full advantage of it. They were near the Dallas Convention Center, stuntin' hard. The strip resembling the scene in *Boyz-n-the-Hood* where the rival's girl asked Cube, "Could we just have a good time?" Only, the girls here were showing way more skin. And instead of lowriders, most of the cars you saw were old schools and foreigns.

200 stood posted in front of his white Aston. The Twinz' matching red Range Rover Sports were a few feet away. He was shirtless with three small gold chains over his tatted skin. His purple designer shorts fell to his shins. And there were all types of colors in his expensive shoes. The Twinz were looking like money too. But it seemed 200 was the most magnetic of the bunch.

"Bro, I'm tellin' you," he spoke to the Twinz. "This shit here so live. I swear it seem like it ain't nothing but hoes in this bitch."

"Speaking of which," Shocka said, eyes falling to someone who was just his type. He slowed the blushing girl and put his mack down.

Meanwhile, 200 and Zilla began to make small talk. They were mentioning how some of these girls' outfits should be illegal, when an uproar rose from the crowd bringing the conversation to a halt. They stepped to the curb to see what

GET IT IN SLUGS | B. STALL

had everyone's attention and there it was, a Maybach with the top cut back like a convertible. It dripped hood and class all at the same time. It was trailed by a Rolls Royce truck and a Lambo truck. And they all were tastefully customized in some way. 200 saw one of the occupants inside the Maybach.

"Ain't this a bitch."

"What? You seeing the same thing I'm seeing?"

"Yeah. This hoe ass nigga, Buck."

In that instant, he and Buck locked eyes. Buck stood inside the slow-rolling Maybach and acknowledged him with a salute. But it seemed fake to him, more like a "fuck you." This was crazy because he knew he didn't fuck with Buck. But it was like Buck was making it apparent now that he didn't fuck with him neither. 200 gave him a subtle head nod, thinking, *it's all good. We know where that stash house at now, nigga. So we gon' see who making a spectacle when this shit all said and done.*

"Damn, Two. I feel for that nigga," Zilla said. "I could see it in yo eyes, you ready to make that bitch nigga bleed."

Shocka walked back over with his phone in his hand and a smile on his face. But when he saw the looks on theirs, he immediately absorbed their angst.

"Yo, did I miss something?"

"Nothing important," 200 answered. "Buck was just making it known that he was ready for his funeral."

While 200 sulked in silence, Shocka reached in his pocket then offered up a much-needed blunt. It seemed to serve its purpose. And after about twenty minutes, the fellas were back to enjoying the festive event.

"So what's up? Y'all want to hit up the main stage or what?" Shocka asked.

This is where the car show held its famous concert series. Performing this year was NBA Young Boy, MoneyBagg Yo, Jene Aíko and a few homegrown acts, Yella Beezy and Z-Ro.

"I do but they prolly ain't gon' let me in with this," 200 patted his shorts. He didn't care about being out on bond for a pistol. He wasn't going anywhere without that strap.

"Parking lot pimpin' it is then," Shocka conceded. Which really wasn't any consolation. The strip was jumpin' just as hard as the happenings inside the event.

They all got back to posting in front of their whips. A little while later when they were debating about whether Miami or Vegas was a better spot to kick it, something caught 200's attention. It came in the form of a bad yella bone. The girl had that glow like the girl Nu-Nu in the movie, *ATL*. She even had the same taste for high fashion because all of her clothes were designer.

"Dang, you just gon' push through without saying hi or nothing?" 200 teased to get her attention.

Her big pretty eyes met his. "I didn't know I was obligated to."

"I mean, you're not," 200 said, stepping to her. "But it would be nice if you did." Instead of giving her too much time to think, he continued to put his press down. "I haven't seen you around. What's your name?"

She pointed at the gold and diamond-encrusted charm sitting in between her luscious breasts. "Queen."

"Queen?" 200 repeated. "What's that? Like your Instagram moniker?"

"Noo...that's what my parents named me."

"Oh, that's dope. I get it, 'cause I can see traits of a Queen in you," he complimented. And he wasn't even tryna gas her. There was something about the way she walked, talked and stood. It was all sexy as hell. She easily stood out to him over the sea of girls at this event. He made his mind up right then that he wasn't leaving here without her.

"You should get it tatted right here," Queen's fuchsia nails found his neck. Then she gave him this adorable smile and suddenly walked off.

"Hold up, ma," 200 said, softly grabbing her waist. He let go of her heart-shaped hips. But now they were face-to-face with each other and he was all in her mix. "I guess since I didn't get your number, we might as well start the date I planned right now."

Queen just looked at him and smiled. She found his charm irresistible. "What are you talking about?" she asked.

200 pulled her hand. "Come over here. Lemme tell you all about it." They posted in front of his Aston and spent the better part of an hour getting to know each other. 200 felt like they'd been friends all his life. From her looks to her vibe, he hadn't run across many girls like Queen before. He felt like this car show was definitely worth the trip. Not only did he get to see Buck, but he also found somebody he wanted to keep around.

"So, tell me something," 200 said. "Which do you think is a better spot to kick it in, Miami or Vegas?"

Queen's sweet voice answered after some thought.

"Mmm…Vegas."

"Let's go."

"Right now?"

"Right now."

"Are you serious?" Shock was evident on Queen's pretty face.

200 grabbed her hand. "Serious as a heart attack."

***

There was a lot of smacking noises and naughty laughter being made inside the uber-deluxe suite at the Bellagio in Vegas.

200 brought Queen to this two-thousand-dollar-a-night piece of heaven after they tried their hand at the casino and ate a five-star meal of Queen's choosing. He did all these things to make her feel special. Now as they laid on the

oversized round bed half naked, it seemed Queen wanted to return the favor.

"Oh shit," 200 said, watching Queen pour champagne on his stomach. "What you doin'?"

Queen looked at him and smiled. "Just having fun." Then she whipped her curly hair over her shoulder and began to slurp up the champagne from everywhere it ran. Her wet tongue worked like a feather as she licked his abs and his side, sending tickling sensations that made him push down unmanly sounds.

"Hold on," 200 protested.

But Queen was bad as she wanted to be and the beauty wasn't stopping until she got what she wanted. She slurped the champagne that soaked through his Versace briefs. Her mouth was brushing his dick like she was actually giving him head. Then she pulled his boxers back and gave him the real deal.

"Got damn, girl. You a fool wit it." 200 stared down as she gave him some of that top notch throat.

This was a side to Queen that most niggas didn't get to know. But if you brought the freak out of her she absolutely owned that shit. Her motto was, *Ain't no bitch fuckin' with me.* And she was on a real live mission right now to show it.

Queen moaned while she sucked him as the sight of his muscle helped her get in her own zone. She was looking even prettier with that dick in her mouth. But if she thought she was gon' have all the fun, she had another thing coming.

"Stand up for a second, ma."

"Hmm..." She slowed.

"Yeah, stand up and take that shit off while you at it," he told her, referring to her black lace bra and panty set. He could already see hints of her nipples and kitty before she came out of her clothes. Then when she tossed them aside, the sight of her naked instantly put her in his top five.

"I got an idea," he said, hustling off to grab the gold bottle of Ace of Spades. When he came back, he challenged her.

"We 'bout to do this sixty-nine thing and see who could make who tap out first."

Queen thought of her superb skills. "I'm game. Breakfast on the loser."

"You ain't said nothin," 200 boasted, following her soft ass towards the plush round bed. As she climbed atop the bed, he took a big boy swig of the champagne then quickly followed suit. He scooted back then leaned on his elbows, allowing her to push her thick high yellow curves directly towards him. He licked his lips. Her pussy looked even prettier from the back. Taking the bottle of champagne, he poured some directly down the crack of her ass. After he was satisfied with the visual, he sat the bottle down and went to work.

"...Mmm," Queen moaned, becoming distracted by the feel of his tongue. 200 cupped her ass and buried his face in it, real nasty-like. He could feel her feather-like tongue going to work on him. But he just kept eatin' the pussy like at the finish line was a mil' ticket. After about five minutes, both of their bodies were turning up. 200 felt sensations build up as his dick throbbed, but Queen's pussy only seemed to get wetter. He continued to lap at her pussy, making it messy, until seconds later she was screaming louder and beating on the bed.

"Okay..."

"Okay, what?"

"You won," she pouted, feeling the rush. She had already come once. And her pussy was too sensitive to take anymore.

200 chuckled knowingly. But seeing her in such a submissive state seemed to bring out the savage in him. Now he was ready to take control of that monkey. "Scoot over," he told her. Then he moved behind her and positioned her on all fours. Her face was down and her juiciness drove him wild as it sat in the air. He tapped his dick along her ass like a paddle. Then he opened her ass cheek just a hair and suddenly pushed in.

Queen grabbed ahold of the sheets as he thrusted her ass towards her perspiring back. She was takin' that dick like a champ as she tried to match his strokes. She began to grab the sheets tighter. "Mmm…fuck!"

Chapter 17

200 and Queen had only spent a day in Vegas. But they spent the last two in the D, glued at the hip. They went on more expensive dates, got to know each other's likes and dislikes. Queen told him about her affluent upbringing, while 200 told her an expurgated version of his struggles coming up. But for the most part, the bulk of their time was spent fuckin'.

Queen came over to the kitchen island and placed the brunch that she had delivered atop the sparkling granite. They were back at her new suburban home, where just hours ago, they played their little tap-out game and once again, she lost.

"Here," Queen said with a counterfeit attitude.

"You look good bringing me food," 200 teased, opening his tray of chicken, waffles and cheese eggs.

Queen sat on one of the chic wooden stools next to him. "Bringing you food? I thought I looked good being your food."

"Yeah, that too."

They shared a laugh then a kiss. And as the sun shined through her overhead window, Queen answered 200's question about how she started her haircare line. Their chemistry was organic and they seemed to be on the same wave about a lot of things. The twenty-four-year-old was cute and caked up. She was definitely his type of bitch.

"Oh yeah, while it's on my mind, lemme show you this," 200 remembered, fishing out his phone. He pulled up a picture of Jaylen, who was wearing a University of Texas t-shirt. "That's my brother right there. He just became the youngest person to ever accept an athletic scholarship from UT."

"Aww, look at Mr. Handsome," she cooed. "Is that the brother you was talking 'bout?"

"Yeah, that's my only brother," 200 corrected her. "He thought I would be mad that he made the decision without me. But I was just happy that he stayed close enough to home for our mom to see him play."

"Well, I think that's too cute. You know, you guys' relationship. I could really tell by the way you talk about him that you two are really close. And I'd be willing to bet that you'll do just about anything for him."

If only she knew. As she began to tell him about how she dropped out of UT, his thoughts drifted. He was closer than ever now to buying a house for his mom. He had about one hundred twenty thousand stashed to the side for her. And at two o'clock, he was scheduled to do a walk-through with the realtor on a two-hundred-thousand-dollar home. Not only that, but his goons were keeping close tabs on Buck. He normally stopped at his million-dollar stash house once a week. And it was around that time now, his plan was coming together.

"Are you done with this?" Queen asked, snapping him out of his daze.

200 looked at the scraps on his Styrofoam tray. "Yeah, I'm good."

Queen reached over him and grabbed the trash, and the scent of her pomegranate skin seemed to do something to him. He felt his snake slither as he watched her throwing everything away. She was wearing her hair down and was in a pink t-shirt, a designer number that stopped right at the crease of her juicy ass. He wondered if she wore shit like this on purpose, because the easy access that it provided was making him want her. He glanced from her gaping yellow legs to his dripped-out timepiece, tryna see if they had enough time for a real quick session. *Damn, it's 1:10 now and I gotta meet with the realtor at 2:00.* He knew tryna get it in would be pushing it. But Queen had that agua that he just couldn't get enough of.

He stalked over to where she stood, then gently twisted her hair around his hand, pulling her back. The tease of his lips quickly found her collar as he pushed her t-shirt right over her round ass and those cute lil panties.

"200," Queen panted. "What are you doin'? I thought you had somewhere to be?"

He pushed her over the counter so her ass would be hiked towards him, and as he pulled her panties to the side, he angled his dick before rushing it inside. Screams and moans filled the air. "You was lookin' too good, ma. I needed that shit."

***

200 arrived at his walk-through about ten minutes late. But the saleswoman greeted him as if he was right on time. "Do you drink?" she asked, holding a bottle of red wine and two flutes.

"Normally, I don't, but I'm sure most men make an exception when it comes to you," he flirted.

The saleswoman was slim and statuesque, and you really couldn't tell if she was Hispanic or white. Her yellow pantsuit didn't do much to compliment her body. But she was such a beautiful woman that he was sure she sold houses based on that alone. She passed him a drink, and they toasted, clinking their glasses.

"First drink in your new home," she spoke prophetically. They began to do a semi-tour as she told him about some of the features of the home. 200 stopped in front of the fireplace in the living room, then looked at the vaulted ceiling. He already felt like this house was the one when he first took a picture of it. Now being inside it, he could see his family making it a home.

"I really want this," he told her. "You're asking two, right?"

"Well, low two's," she corrected him. "You know, with closing and fees, it should be right around two-ten."

200 followed her drift. He knew that extra ten thousand came from an under the table, all-cash deal, Head put in place.

"So, what you think?" she asked, looking around the house. The question made his thoughts flash to Buck. The seven-figure lick they were plotting would surely put him over the hump. He could practically see Buck fearful and begging for his life. Boom!

"I'm definitely interested," 200 told her. "But I got a few things that I need to handle first. Let me get back at you after I take care of that." They toasted once more to future business.

Chapter 18

Zilla stared through the window of 200's dated Acura in the direction of Buck's Oak Cliff stash house. He was unusually quiet. He was too busy sulking about the fact that he felt this was a dry run. For the past few nights, they parked in front of this unoccupied home, waiting for hours and in one instance, nearly all day in hopes of snatching Buck up so he could lead them to the stash. But suppose he never showed? Suppose he didn't really have all this cash that 200 thought he did?

"Aye yo, bro," Zilla said to Shocka. "Do you really think it's as much money in there as 200 be sayin'?" 200 had stepped out to take a closer look at the house.

"I don't see why it wouldn't be. You know 200 like a mastermind when it comes to plottin' licks. That boy a fool wit it and he always come through."

"I wouldn't say always. It's been times that he ain't come through before."

"When?"

Zilla spotted 200's shadowy figure. "Oh shit, here he comes." Nervousness filled the cabin as they watched 200 rush from the murky fog of the sidewalk to the driver's side of the car. His breaths were slightly labored when he hopped inside.

"What you see?" Zilla asked, watching 200 shed his hood.

"Not much. The home seemed quiet and I didn't hear any sounds like a TV or radio to let you know someone was inside."

Zilla looked back at Shocka condescendingly, like, *"What I tell you."* This was furthering Zilla's case that they were on a bogus mission. He didn't really see the logic in stalking a dude for a month. He felt like their energy could be better used somewhere else. But this was 200's ship and he was the captain, he mentally mocked him. "So what's the play?" he asked, already knowing the answer.

"Let's just wait it out for a minute to see if the nigga come through."

Go figure.

Zilla thought 200's infatuation with Buck was borderline obsession. Was it *really* about the money? Or was it personal? Five weeks of stalking? He weighed. Yeah, it was personal. Zilla sighed, then fell back.

About half an hour later, the squad was still focused on the house when out of nowhere some high beams swept through the car. It made them conscious of the guns they had in the whip and the danger they were facing if this was the police. After a few stress filled seconds, the light left the whip. But the incident was a wake-up call to their complacent behavior. They had been out here too long and knew they needed to shake the spot. 200 quickly started the car and got in traffic. Then he got busy thinking about what time he would be back here tomorrow.

Chapter 19

Present Day

"We should prolley roll, cuz," Zilla suggested from the backseat, conscious of his surroundings and growing a little antsy. But 200 squinted through the murky clouds at a pair of headlights coming down the street.

"Hold on," 200 said, peeping the car's silhouette. "This might be him." *Or he hoped.* The Highland Hills hardhead had been on a mission over the past year plus, preying on local dope boyz and racking up a serious body count in the process. His brazen actions put the streets on notice and it was all in hopes of buying a home for his mom. At least that's what he claimed. He wanted her to raise his promising young brother in a better neighborhood. Though most of the money that crossed his hands were usually squandered on extravagant gifts, expensive cars, clothes—mostly that high dolla shit, vacations, strip clubs and supporting his gambling habit.

But this was different. This was a stash house that belonged to an underground legend, and after doing his due diligence, he learned that there was over a million dollars cash inside it. Something that would surely put him over the hump. The type of trap this revered jackboy had to have.

Seeing 200 sit a mask atop his unkempt taper, the nerves in the car became palpable. You might as well have said the police were on the block.

"So, is that him?" Shocka asked from the passenger side as he began to study the car too.

200 put a choppa on his lap the size of a small pole. He didn't readily answer. He continued to squint his beady eyes at the approaching car until it hit the lights and pulled to the curb slightly past the house. The occupant hopped out but it was a female and not the dude they'd been casing the home for.

"Nah, it ain't him," he said in a whisper of defeat.

They were about to tuck their guns and call it a night until another car pulled up directly behind the first. He watched as dude put his feet on the damp pavement then looked around suspiciously before proceeding to the house. He could tell that cocky strut from a mile away. "Yo, that's that bitch ass nigga Buck right there. Mount up," 200 said. Pistols began to click and clack inside the car, while all the car's dark-dressed occupants looked to 200 as if he were their general. And when he gave his command, they masked up and jumped out.

"C'mon, it's go time."

200 quietly shut the door and the Twinz followed suit. They all crept towards the unassuming pair, but 200 walked swifter, taking the lead. He began to zone in on the back of Buck's bald head thinking, *yeah nigga, it's on now.* The pair were dressed like they'd just left the bar. Only now, he was about to make them wish they would have stayed.

Buck's loud voice echoed through the still of the night. They entered the house without a care. But before they could close the door good, 200's foot came barreling down, knocking whoeva was behind it to the floor.

They stormed inside.

"Bitch, don't move! Stay down!" These were some of the commands that rose over panicked screams.

Despite all the commotion, 200 peeped Buck reaching for his waist and butted him in the face with the choppa, knocking him flat on his back. He seemed to take pride in all the blood that ran from his eyelid. "Now, I said don't move," he warned. "And that goes for you too, Slim Goodie. Or I'ma make sure yo ass be the first to go." The horrified woman held her hands over her brown skin. She was clearly jittery and worried that she wouldn't be able to control her dry heaving.

"Look," Buck said, holding his eye. "You don't even realize what you're getting yourself into. I'll give you one chance to leave. And I'll forget this ever happened."

From the way he talked, you would'a swore he was in control.

"One chance, huh? You hear this clown?" 200 looked at the guys. Then he pointed to Buck's pocket. "Yo, take the pistol off this pussy."

The sheer audacity that Buck was making demands ruffled his feathers. He trained the choppa on his chest. He wanted to make himself clear. "Yo, the only way I'm leaving is with the stash I came here fo'."

"Stash?" Buck frowned in confusion.

"Yeah, we all know about the million dollars you got stashed in this bitch."

"A mil, sheit. Somebody musta gave you the wrong address."

200 snarled under his mask. "Well, we gon' see 'bout that." He began to storm in the direction of the girl in the corner. He knew she meant something to Buck by the way he seemed focused on her. He snatched her up by her sandy brown dreads, causing a yelp. The woman feared this deranged man was about to do her harm.

"Please don't hurt me...what did I do?" With every step they took, she seemed to resist.

"Bro, don't let them do anything to me. Please, stop them!"

Oh, this is his sister, 200 thought. Well that's even better. He clutched her dreads tighter and forced her into the kitchen.

Buck looked at the Twinz with concern in his eyes. "Yo, what the fuck is he doing to my sister?"

"It ain't what he doin'," Shocka spoke. "It's what you doin'. He asked you where the stash at, but you wanna play dumb. And because of that, yo sista is in this position."

A few seconds passed with Buck in thought. Then an unearthing cry reached his ear. "Aaah!"

"Say…hold on, man, what the fuck." Buck tried to get up. But Zilla sent a boot right to his chest and knocked him back on the floor. Seeing the pistols aimed at him held him for an instant. Then he heard some more of her unearthing cries and he thought dude was 'bout to kill her. "Hell nah, man. Let her go," he grew defiant. If their parents taught them anything, it was to fend for each other. He tried again to get up but was met with a barrage of kicks to the head and chest from both Twinz. It would have stymied him, but her hysterical pleas continued.

"Ow…owww!" she shouted. "Please stop. Oh, my God. Buck, help! He's gonna kill me!" Her sobs that she didn't do anything, filled the air until suddenly you couldn't hear her anymore.

Buck felt like, *fuck this shit.* He tried to rush to his feet, clashing with the Twinz, until a pistol butted him in the head, knocking him out cold. He sat groggily on the carpet like a boxer who was under the count. It wasn't until he grew conscious of the Twinz cussing that his faintness began to wane. He blinked only to notice a black pistol mere inches from his face.

"Now get up again, Billy Badass, and I'ma go in there and kill yo sista myself," Shocka warned.

A light coat of tears fought through the anger in Buck's eyes. He had to force himself to fall back just for the sake of his sister. He hoped that she was alright. And if they let him live, he promised to find out who did this and kill 'em himself. His voice was hoarse with sadness when he spoke.

"Did he kill her? Is she alive?"

"Aye, come back here, y'all!" 200 yelled from the kitchen "I'ont know," Shocka told Buck. "Let's go see for ourselves." When Buck tried to stand up, he told him, "Nah, nigga. I want you to crawl. You put your own sister under the gun. A nigga like you don't deserve to walk."

Buck crawled on the dated carpet in his designer apparel as they made their way towards the refurbished kitchen. He was listening for any sounds that may soothe the fears that she wasn't dead. But when he entered the kitchen and saw her lying in a pool of blood, it was more than his heart could bear.

"Mia," he mourned. He looked at 200, who was kneeling over her bound and gagged body, holding a bloody knife. "She's dead?"

"Nah, but she will be if you don't come up off that stash." 200 hit Mia on the shoulder. "Turn over and let your brother see that you're alive." She turned over to face Buck but alive is about all she was. She had deep stab wounds on her arm and thigh. And the normal cool her face sported was replaced with great angst.

Buck felt like shit seeing her like this. Mia was a good girl, a student at Texas Southern who accompanied him to a comedy show because he was welcoming her back home. He knew his brother would kill him if he let something happen to her. He was the one who asked to put something in her car, when she literally was coddled and sheltered from this part of their lifestyle. He contemplated giving the money up. This was going against everything he stood for. But this was Mia, the baby of the family and no amount of money was worth her life.

"Let's say if I give you the stash," Buck semi-offered. He figured since they were all wearing masks they would let them live.

"If?" 200 asked, raising the knife. He threatened to bring it down on Mia. Pressure was known to burst pipes.

"No...no...no...no...no," Buck pleaded. "Don't do that. I'ma give you the money. But could you promise to let us live?"

Even though you couldn't see 200's face, you felt his assurance.

"You give me the stash and that's a promise. We'll take the bread and be on our way."

Taking him at his word, Buck got up and led 200 and Zilla to what appeared to be a child's room. It looked like a haven for a princess but it was really a den for drug money. Buck moved past the small bed, then on to a playhouse. He pushed the playhouse to the side then looked at the beige carpet.

"If you pull back the carpet from the corner, you could pretty much feel the false bottom. Then just pick up the tile and you'll see a duffle bag under there."

This was information that got 200's adrenaline pumping. He swiftly moved to the corner while Zilla held Buck at bay. As he removed the bag from the secret compartment, Buck watched with intrigue as 200 thumbed through its contents. He hoped that he would be content with a quarter million dollars and leave. But as his head bolted up towards Buck, he knew he had a problem.

200 leveled the choppa and began to storm towards Buck. "You playin', nigga?"

Buck thought of how he went in on his sister.

"Nah, of course not. I got anotha bag in the house. I just led you to this one first."

"Walk, nigga," 200 instructed. He poked Buck on his stocky shoulder blade with the choppa to get his feet moving. He seemed to wonder what type of elaborate set-up Buck was going to lead them to next. He was thinking somewhere like the wall or the ceiling. But he was a little surprised that Buck led them back to the kitchen. He pointed past where Shocka had Mia hemmed up by the stove.

"It's in the oven," Buck told them. He had prepared the bag earlier so they could take it to another spot.

Anxiously, 200 walked to the oven and opened it, discovering a large black duffel bag that weighed about sixty pounds. When he pulled it out, light dust rose as the bag dropped to the floor. He kneeled down and opened it. *Hallelujah*, he thought. Inside was a sea of large bills, blue and green. He zipped the bag back up content that he was staring at a mil.

"You know, Buck, I tried to tell you before that a nigga like me had bull nuts," 200 taunted, starting towards him.

Buck mouthed the word, *bull nuts* as if he were confused. But when 200 removed the mask from over his tatted face, it all started coming back. *The dice game.* The unspoken static between them. He stared into his eyes. He knew he was fucked.

"Say, kill the girl," 200 yelled to Shocka, who obliged by pushing his .40 into her dreads. B'ough! B'ough!

"No! We had a deal," Buck cried.

200 quieted him with a quick barrage of bullets to his body and face. Bop! Bop! Bop! Bop! Bop! He stared with a scowl as Buck's bloody body laid slumped against the fridge. "Bitch ass nigga," he spewed.

But his emotional victory was short lived because bullets began to blaze from behind him. The choppa leaped from his hand and his body lurched forward as the surprising shots continued to land. Three shots hit his back and another grazed his neck, making him sprawl on his face against the floor a few feet away from Buck. He laid still like a possum but he could hear everything around him.

"Man, what the…you killed the homie?" Shocka asked.

"Bro, fuck this bitch ass nigga. Now we got the bread to ourselves."

"Yo, that's some bullshit, Bro. We supposed to be a team."

"Are you gon' stand there and keep bitchin'? Or you gon' help me grab this money so we could leave?" Zilla asked.

200 heard the bustle of their feet as they moved around him. The pain made it troublesome for him to stay still.

Though he did so long enough to hear the front door slam. It took a few more seconds for him to build up the courage to open his eyes. Then he sat up, raised his hoodie, and began to unfasten the straps of his Kevlar vest. Just doing this caused him to hiss in pain. He was fortunate that these were mere bruises and even more fortunate that he followed his intuition and wore the vest. Coming into tonight, he knew that shit could get ugly. Buck's crew was said to be formidable, and he wasn't about to walk into the unknown unprepared.

With as much haste as he could muster, 200 took the bulletproof vest off and saw the brass slugs lodged in its material. That's when he noticed the blood around the left collar. He patted the side of his neck. His hand came away crimson red. "Fuck, I got nicked. I gotta get the fuck up outta here." Seeing the dead bodies just a few feet away seemed to light a fire under his ass.

He took his ski mask and wiped up the droplets of blood his wound left. Then he glanced around to look for his choppa and didn't see it. They took his gun and his money and left him on his dick. *That's some hoe ass shit*, he thought about the Twinz' betrayal as he scurried towards the door. But that was the least of his worries right now. He walked into the dark of the night, which looked like a ghost town. He didn't see his Acura anywhere in sight and he had no way home.

Fuck!

Chapter 20

Sabrina was cozied up with PG on an outdoor daybed, watching the waterproof TV on the terrace of his gated home. It was some playa shit, as PG referred to it. Birds were chirping, the gray skies were giving a comforting breeze and neither of their kids were around to mess things up. Sabrina nestled further underneath his stocky frame. They were doing what they did when they weren't sexing, kicking back and enjoying each other's company.

PG had grown into more than just a close friend over these last four months. His patient listening is what allowed her to get through this ordeal with 200 and really enjoy the stages of getting to know him. She learned that he was a really good cook who loved sports and raised one son by himself, just like her. He told her about his two siblings, and how important family is. But she still hadn't cracked what he did outside of his "recycling business." She had her suspicions and judging from the size of his home, he was either selling a lot of pallets or using them to package something else. She picked a piece of lint out of his bushy beard. "200 called the other day."

"You answer?" PG asked.

"Nope. I didn't feel like being bothered with him or any of his bullshit."

"I don't blame you. A nigga like him don't deserve your attention. In fact, I'm starting to want it all to myself."

The beauty blushed at his smoothness.

"See, that's what I love about you, you're a good listener. You just let me vent without complaining. And it's really helping me get over this."

PG peered off into her alluring eyes. "You love something about me?"

Sabrina entertained what he was implying. She stared deeper in his eyes, stroking their connection. "Yep." They shared a kiss. Then PG's hand began to roam the split of her long yellow dress. He pulled her warm body atop of his right on the thickness of his growing erection.

"Is that the only thing that you love about me?" he teased.

Since they've been vibin' she also learned that he had a sex drive that was out of this world.

"Boy you a mess," she said, then leaned over and kissed him.

Their kisses started out affectionate but grew more passionate by the moment.

PG knew that he wanted to get it in and was doing everything in his power to get Sabrina ready. They hadn't sexed in two days. But for him it felt like two months. He slid his hands under her dress until he cupped two handfuls of her soft, succulent ass. That's when he noticed she wasn't wearing any panties. "Shit," he said, surprised. He tried to hurry his piece out but suddenly stopped when he heard a name coming from the TV that rang a bell...Golliday.

He began to listen to the slender, white newswoman more intently.

Jamel and JaMia Golliday were reportedly headed to this Oak Cliff home when armed assailants forced them inside...

"Hold on," PG said to Sabrina, who was kissing his neck. He rushed the confused cutie off of him and then ran to the large TV. The lust he felt was now gone. A new, more gloomy emotion was in the air, call it dread—dread provoked by the familiar image of his main stash house. The neighbors that he recognized—the surrealness of the news being there. *Please don't say what I think you're about to say,* he pleaded silently to the reporter. His heart beat wildly with alarm in anticipation of the inevitable.

...in an unfortunate twist, the police found both bodies riddled with bullets and the female victim suffering from multiple stab wounds. The police believe that they were possibly the targets of a drug-related robbery. The two were pronounced dead at the scene.

Everything around PG seemed to fade to black as whatever normalcy he had was flipped on its head. *Am I really seeing this?* He hoped like hell that his mind was playing tricks on him or this was a really bad dream. But there was the large stone stash house he had recently refurbished. And there was the unexpected touch of Sabrina's comforting hand.

"Are you OK?" she asked, seeing the distress on his face. Her words seem to bring it all home. He fell to his knees as pained tears filled his eyes.

"Nah...hell nah. This can't be," he cried.

"What?" Sabrina asked as she began to soothe his back.

"They killed them...that was my lil brother and sister, Buck and Mia."

"But I thought you said your brother managed your recycling business. They were talking like that was a robbery that had something to do with drugs."

Sabrina's naivety made PG's sobs pause for a very brief second. He looked into her eyes and told her the truth. "Look, baby, I'm a Golliday...that hustlin' street shit is what we do. But Mia, she's a good girl. She didn't deserve to go out like this." He fell over and grabbed her ankle as he really began to bawl.

"PG, get up." she tried to get him out of his defeated position. "And stop crying like that. You're gonna make me cry too."

After several failed attempts, she finally got him to at least straighten up. This was hard for him to comprehend. The news struck him like lightning. He searched her eyes for empathy. "I just don't understand," is what he tried to say. But the only thing that came out was a sorrow filled, "I—" He clung to her with all he had, tears decorating the midriff of her dress.

"It's going to be okay," she said, hugging him with equal ferocity. But her words were feeble in consoling him. The wind picked up as they swayed and cried together.

Chapter 21

Dealing with his own problems on the other side of town, 200 sat between Queen's legs on the carpet of his swanky apartment. There was nothing but medical supplies by their side and as Queen tended to the flesh wound on his neck, he hissed from the pressure she applied.

"Damn girl, I thought you said you knew what you was doin'."

Queen continued to hold the medical gauze in place as her yellow baby face filled with fake attitude.

"I do," she countered. "My mother was in hospice for twenty years. I done watched her do this a thousand times before."

"I sho' hope so," he teased.

"Boy, whateva, just stay still."

Queen opened up a strong green bottle of anesthesia. While she attended to his wound, 200 fell into a dark space. Moment by moment, all of her infectious joy withered away. Now all he could think about was getting at these bitch ass Twinz. He told himself anybody, including their peeps, could get it since they called themselves wanting to pull some fuck shit. He was wondering where the niggas might be when he felt Queen leaning over his shoulder.

"200. Did you hear me?"

"Yeah… I heard you," his voice broke with lies. "My mind just on some other shit right now."

She began to gather all of the medical supplies off the carpet. "I asked how'd you end up getting shot in the first place."

"Why?" his face screwed. "So I can tell you what happened and you get scared and quit fuckin' with me?"

Queen wasn't expecting that response.

"Whoa, sorry I asked."

"Nah, don't be sorry. You wanted to know, so I'ma tell you. Some niggas tried to rob me. A few bullets missed but one ended up hittin' me in the neck. There. You scared now? You gon' find an excuse to run your little prissy self back to the suburbs?"

This was the first hint of adversity they had in their young friendship. But Queen knew he was frustrated and didn't take it personally.

"Look, I don't know what your impression of me is," she stared in his face. "But I know who you are. The whole city does. And I would have never let you in if I wasn't willing to ride."

"Yeah…yeah. Tell me anything," he brushed her off. But Queen persisted, grabbing his wrist and staring in his eyes with more sincerity.

"I'm serious, 200. I'm really down for you."

"Well, we gon' see," 200 said, watching her kiss his tatted chest. It quelled his fire for a minute then his attention went right back to gettin' at these Twinz.

***

"Ju, man…you always gettin' at these fat girls," Jaylen teased as they walked through the decrepit streets of Highland Hills.

"She wasn't fat. She just had a lil meat on her."

"A lil meat. Bro, ol girl was built like Precious before *Empire*."

"Nah, she wasn't that big."

"Well, she wasn't far from it."

"Man, you just mad 'cause I beat you to it."

"There was no competition for her. Trust me, she was all you."

They laughed for a minute as they continued to stroll through the cuts and corners of their stomping grounds. They talked about Jaylen's young season, girls, then more football before Jaylen suddenly had to take a leak.

"Say, I'ma duck off in this alley real quick," he told Ju, holding his crotch. He would have stopped on the side of the house. But he scurried a little further since the fall sun still showed through the weak clouds. As he did his thing, an image of ol girl rose, making him chuckle. *Ju crazy*, he thought. She wasn't even no cute big girl or nothing.

He finished doing his thing then began to head back towards front street. From this distance, he caught a glimpse of Ju's blue hoodie through the slits in the wooden fence and was ready to ride down on him again about ol girl, when some contentious words reached his ear. It was like the growl of a predator before it attacks its prey.

"That was you, pussy. You told that nigga 200 where I stay."

"Yo, whateva you and 200 had going on, that was on y'all. I ain't have nothing to do with that shit," he heard Ju cop a plea.

Jaylen's heart began to race at the mention of his brother's name. There was tension in the air. He could feel that it was about to go down. But still he rushed to where Ju was ready to get out there for his guy. Though that whole sentiment changed when he saw Ju at the wrong end of the chrome fo-fifth.

"Oh shit," Jaylen said, swirling back around the fence. As he tried to steady his breathing, ripples of fear filled his heart. Just beyond the fence, Cap, the guy he fought, and another guy had his close friend at gunpoint. He yearned to go out there and help make Ju's bond. But it was like 200's words willed their way in his head. *You gotta be smarter than that. You can't be hanging out in the hood. You got too much going for yaself. And you know how these Highland Hills niggas be.* Jaylen had always known that he was from the hood. But he had never seen the ills of it play out firsthand.

When Cap's threatening voice filled the air, Jaylen peeped through the hole in the fence in a surreal state.

"Fuck you lying for, nigga? You did tell 'em," Cap barked.

"On the real, I ain't lyin'. I swear it wasn't me."

"You hear this pussy?" his boy asked.

"Yeah, I hear him," Cap frowned.

From here, everything seemed to move slower for Jaylen. He watched the alarmed expression on Ju's face as he began to backpedal. Then when his hands raised in surrender all hell broke loose.

F'ough! F'ough! F'ough! F'ough! F'ough!

"N—" Jaylen barely covered his mouth before he started to scream. He stood there for a minute frozen in shock. Then it seemed the killaz began to look for the sound of the noise, making him dash in the opposite direction.

***

200 felt a nip in the wind and heard a grumble from the dark clouds as he hid in the bushes in the back of Zilla's baby mama's house. He was out there bad, in all black, not giving a fuck who saw him. All he wanted to do was smash one of these bitch ass Twinz.

After watching the home for a good minute, 200 thought he needed a closer look, which caused him to leave the bushes. The grumble grew louder as he stalked along the warped siding near the perimeter by the kitchen. Although it was dark inside, he could have sworn that he just saw the curtains move. "C'mon, bitch nigga. If you in there, then show ya face," he groaned.

GET IT IN SLUGS | B. STALL

There was embers in his eyes that seemed to flame each time he thought of these fake ass niggas' betrayal. Never mind the over one million cash they took, or the countless times he done broke bread, his own potnas tried to off him. And for that, bodies were gon' to have to fall.

200 began to creep along the side of the house near the bedroom to see if there was any activity in there. He pulled his hoodie tighter then brought an attentive ear to the wall. Just when he heard the whispers from a TV, a passing car slowed, then suddenly, without warning, its overhead lights blared. This made his heartbeat 100 times faster because the only cars he knew with these lights were the muthafuckin' police. Frozen in shock, he studied the car wondering was that them. Then a similar car swerved up with its lights off from the opposite direction. *Sho' the fuck is*, he thought, then skedaddled off.

"Aye, don't move!" one of the officers yelled.

But 200 was already running like his life depended on it.

"Hey, you. Stop!" another one barked.

Though the heat from the officer's words made him run with more vigor, he was conscious that he was out on bond for a pistol and was a person of interest in at least two homicides. Fuck was they talkin'? Stopping was never an option. He cut through the yard of a pastel-painted home, then darted to the other side across the empty street. He did this again at another home, then ran up a few blocks. There were no officers in sight, apparently, he must've shaken them. But he knew that the laws were in the vicinity because he could hear the hum of their engines gunning.

"Damn," 200 said, hesitating momentarily as he tried to weigh his options. His car was just a block away. But it was too hot to even get to it. He heard the gunning engines of their squad cars getting closer, and hopped the fence then ran through the alley. Zilla's baby mama's house was just a few minutes from his T lady's. So he ran with all he had until he safely made it there. As 200 laid against the door wide eyed and breathing heavily, he took in the familiar comforts of his T lady's home. Little by little his nervous energy began to dwindle. But it didn't fully dissipate until he checked the blinds and saw the coast was clear.

"Fuck," he said, collapsing on the couch. But it wasn't the close call that had him frustrated, he was trippin' off the fact that he didn't get to dome nothing.

200 buried his face in his palm, then let out a deep sigh as reality took a jab at him. The Twinz had beat him on the jux for over a million cash. And now they were nowhere around to feel these problems. He zoned out, staring at the carpet, consummating ways that he was gonna to get them back. Just when his thoughts created a sinister cloud around him, a sniffle reached his ear making the cloud somewhat part. He got up listening harder as he began to follow the sorrow filled sound down the hall. They weren't coming from Renee's room. They were coming from Jaylen's, he noted.

200 subtly knocked, then entered the room. As light from the hall floated inside, it gradually hit a cluttered floor, the bed and a defeated Jaylen, whose clothed body was sprawled across the mattress with pillows flung atop his head. Hearing his troubled cries, 200's heart filled with concern. He sat on the bed next to him.

"Bro, you alright?" he asked. But Jaylen just continued to cry, so he tried to infuse some light into the situation. "Ain't none of these lil girls break my lil brutha heart, did they?"

"Nah," Jaylen corrected. "It ain't nothing like that." He tried to explain what happened but just ended up crying again.

200 placed a comforting hand on his back. "What is it?" Jaylen finally found the strength to sit up. He steadied his breathing and wiped the tears from his face.

"They killed my boy, man," he pouted.

"Ya boy who! Who you talkin' bout, Jaylen?"

He pinched the bridge of his nose before coughing out an answer. "Ju. My friend I used to hang out with from down the street. You know him. Kinda slim. Nappy fro."

200 recognized who he was talking about. "Be posted on the block?"

"Yeah, we was just walking, talking smack when I had to take a leak. Next thing I know, I came back up the alley and Cap 'nem had him at gunpoint. I didn't think they would shoot him though. But seeing the gun, I hurried back around the fence before they could see me." He was imagining it. "You could still see from where I was how scared Ju was. And I started to go back out there, bro. I swear I did! But it was like I could hear you telling me how I needed to be smart and whatnot. But I shouldn't'a left him out there by himself. I shoulda ran and helped." He dropped his head towards the floor.

200 was moved by Jaylen's words. Although he had freakish strength for his age, you could hear his youth when he spoke. He sounded innocent, vulnerable even.

"Nah, you ain't done nothing wrong." 200 massaged his collar. "You did the smartest possible thing. There was nothing you could do."

Generating a smidgen of strength from somewhere, Jaylen added, "They arrested Cap and ol boy too. It's been all over the news."

As Jaylen said this, 200 was thinking about the suburban crib he wanted for Renee. It would have isolated him from the dangers of the hood, his main reason for wanting it. 200 took Jaylen's shoes off and told him to get some rest. He was hoping he could get some too because there were deadly plots unfolding in his head.

Chapter 22

Zilla heard the enthusiastic cheers of Shocka and the invited strippers, as he lowered his face to the coke that sat atop the wet bar. For the past four days, he and his brother had been out here at this rented mansion in Katy, Texas, partying like crazy. No one could tell him that he wasn't rich now. He was doin' it how he always wanted to.

Zilla snorted the line so hard that when he stood, his stocky frame slightly staggered. He felt like he had left earth and took off to the moon. But when he came down, his attention then slowly drifted back to the hard sounds of Pop Smoke, then the sexy lil baddie—and the fact that she was standing in front of him, wearing next to nothing.

"Baby, you alright?" she asked, gliding her hands near his new gleaming gold figaro.

"Yeah, I'm good. That shit right there that real. Why don't you and yo girl go 'head and try some."

As the baddie and her long-haired Latin friend stepped over to the wet bar, Zilla took his elbow and nudged Shocka on the sly.

"Which one you want?" he whispered, looking at them.

Shocka tugged his bushy beard but didn't hesitate long.

"I want that one," he nodded at the long-haired Latin with the tattoo under her butt cheeks. Zilla laughed. His brother seemed to always go for the thick chicks. But he wasn't doing no trippin', he got the prettiest one of the bunch. They were talking on the sly about how they were gonna bust 'em up but cut the conversation short when the girls approached.

"Damn, you wasn't lying. That shit was good," the baddie said as she swung Zilla's way. She had an angel face but this devilish look in her eyes. You could just tell that the coke had her down for whatever. She seemed to have a natural willingness to make him happy. She began to untuck Zilla's white tank top and caress his hairy stomach. Then the phone rang on the counter, somewhat killing his vibe.

Ring... Ring...

"Is that one of y'alls?" asked the long-haired Latin.

"That's mine," Zilla acknowledged. "But let that muthafucka ring, it's good."

He pulled the baddie into him and as her pink painted nails began to travel south, suddenly, the caller hit the phone right back.

"On second thought, give it to me." He wanted to cut the ringer off and tuck it in his pocket so he wouldn't lose it. But when the Latin vixen grabbed the phone, she accidentally hit "Accept."

"Oh shit," she said, quickly passing Zilla the phone.

Noticing the blunder, Zilla smacked his lips. *Ain't this a bitch.* It was the one person he'd been avoiding and it was too late to end the call. He put the phone to his ear and his baby mama was already going off.

"Where the hell you at? And what's all that music in the background?"

"Hold on, Kesha. Let me get out of this car real quick," he lied. After excusing himself from the crowd, he quickly made his way through the Miami-themed living room of the posh estate. It was still a little noisy where he was, so he slid open the glass door and stepped on the green ground by the lake.

"Look Keesh... don't start with that bullshit."

"Don't start, Nugga. Do you have any idea what I've been going through?"

The stress in her voice was accompanied by unexpected sobs. Zilla knew his girl was a trooper. There must have really been something wrong.

"Keesh, is everything alright?" he asked, growing concerned. She took a moment to compose herself, then her cries turned to anger.

"No, everything's not alright. I'm sitting here with your daughter in fear of my life while you runnin' the fuckin streets doing God knows what."

"What the hell do you mean in fear of your life?"

"Exactly what I said," she answered with equal fervor. Then her temperament changed and vulnerability welled inside her. "Baby, I'm scared. The other day I saw someone in the bushes, so I called the police. But he came back."

"Is he there right now?"

"I don't know... I mean, he could be. I saw him like twenty minutes ago. But I just took the baby and I've been hiding in our room ever since."

"Why didn't you just call the police?"

"For what? It didn't scare 200 off last time."

Zilla frowned. "200?"

"Yeah...your friend."

"Nah...nah...nahh—there ain't no way that can be him. Last time I checked, 200 was dead."

Before Kesha could rebut, a resistive Zilla momentarily lost consciousness of their conversation and thought back to the shooting. It was like he was seeing everything in slo-mo. 200's vulnerable body. His extended arm. The loud sparks. The damaging slugs. He even remembered the pool of blood by his head as they rushed out of the house and left him for dead. So ain't no way this could have been 200 she saw. Right? He spent another split second pondering the possibility until Kesha's defiant voice brought him out of his trance.

"Zilla," she called. "Are you listening? He's alive. I know that little beady eyed muthafucka wherever I see him. It's the same 200 that used to mess with my girl. The same one that everybody knows don't fuck around. And he's here stalking our home like he's waiting for a kill. Baby, where the fuck are you at? You need to come home and do something."

"I am…I am…Just calm down." Zilla began to pace. He wasn't trying to hear that 200's alive shit. He wanted to know that fool was dead so he could live happily ever after with the dough. Zilla paced past the sliding glass door until he reappeared with a more distraught look on his face. 200 was known to get at your family members if he couldn't get at you. And now he had a much bigger problem on his hands.

"Babe, look." he stopped pacing. "There's a gun in the closet. I want you to get it out of the shoebox and keep it close by just in case. You and the baby, y'all stay in that room but call the police. Tell them you're scared because you see your ex, walking outside your house with a gun in his hand, trippin'."

"But bae," she pouted.

"No buts, Keesh. Just do it. I'm out in Louisiana right now. I'll be there as soon as I can."

Zilla ended the call but it seemed his troubles had just begun. This crazy motherfucker was on the loose, and he knew he had vengeance on his mind. As the strain began to weigh on him, his shaking head found the site of the artificial lake. It seemed the wind was making its waters picturesque. But the same wind was troubling him. He was worried that 200 was 'bout to do something unpredictable. If it was him, he could handle it. But to his family? Hell nawl. He made a decision right then that was based on fear and desperation. He brought his smart phone to his face then looked around before speaking in a hushed tone.

"Aye, Siri, get me the number to the Dallas Homicide Division."

After the number popped up on his phone, he immediately dialed it. A few anxious seconds later, a disarming voice greeted him.

"Yes, this is Detective Winters speaking."

Zilla covered his mouth, hoping to disguise his voice. "Are you familiar with the story that's been all over the news, the murders on Ledbetter?"

From the other end of the phone, Detective Winters hastily waved *The First 48* camera crew over. "I most certainly am. It's the one where they recently killed the brother and sister."

"Well, consider this your lucky day. I got some news that can help you solve it."

Chapter 23

As Sabrina exited the CVS in the middle of the large shopping complex with her son in tote, she thought, *"Ooh, it's a nice day."* Today was a fall day that could have only happened in Texas. You could still get by in ya summer clothes, and Sabrina wasn't one not to take advantage. She broke out the sexy gray leggings and a white sports bra that unintentionally flaunted her Kardashian-esque curves. Her fine hair and biracial features only complimented her further. Though she probably was the least bit concerned with her outward appearance—it was what was inside that literally had her stopping at CVS.

Sabrina clutched a bag with a pregnancy test in one hand and Lil Jason's hand in the other. She stared into his cute face. *Looks like you may have a little brother or sister soon,* she thought. Although she hadn't taken the test yet, she sensed that she was pregnant. Her cycle was three weeks late. And for the past few months, her and PG had been sexing like crazy without protection. There was no question in her mind as to who the father was. Let's just hope he didn't turn out to be as bummy as her ex.

As they continued towards the car, Sabrina looked down at Lil Jason and saw the striking resemblance to his father, 200. His nose. His head. Those beady eyes. But she didn't see any of the qualities that made her despise him. All she saw was her Poon-Poon and her adorable little man. Her voice grew sweet like she did when she looked at him.

"You hungry?" she asked, smiling as he nodded his head.
"Well, what you wanna eat?"
"Mmm..." he pondered.
"You want nuggets?" she finished for him.
"Yeah, I want that." Lil Jason lit up.

As she was retrieving her car keys, she slightly looked over and saw the shadow of a car moving alongside her. She knew the driver was trying to get her attention and didn't even bother to look over. But when the sound of MO 3 was lowered, a polite voice made her soften up.

"Excuse me, Miss? If you're leaving, can I have that spot?" Sabrina looked inside the new black Benz S class and saw the large man with a smile and confidence of Biggie Smalls.

"This spot?" she questioned. "I'm sure one of these other spots will do." There were empty spaces all over the lot.

"Nah. Actually, this is the one I gotta have."

"Why is that?" Sabrina kept her head straight.

"That way I can get used to pullin' up where you be." Sabrina peeped his game from a mile away, but still couldn't help but laugh.

"Ahh, you see," the driver said. "Got you grinning already." He seemed poised to shoot his shot. But then he looked from her smile to the rearview mirror and it was like he'd seen a ghost. He suddenly sped off without looking back, making a light screech. This seemed to push the fear that he felt directly on Sabrina. She instinctively looked back and saw the flashing lights of two unmarked cars quickly closing in. She tightened the grip on her son's hand, while her soft brown eyes stared at the car, confused. Then she remembered one of the cars, the Ford Taurus, from the last time she was harassed. Now, she was all but ready to let these relentless pigs have it. She fastened Lil Jason safely into the car seat, then stood by her door with her hand on her hip. The husky black man with the razor bumps under his chin was the first to approach.

"Ms. Edwards, can we have a word?" Detective Winters asked. But Sabrina was rather short.

"I thought I told you before that I wasn't talking to you guys. Or should I call my lawyer?"

"You know what, a lawyer might not be such a bad idea, Ms. Edwards. Especially if we're staring at a potential accessory to murder."

"Murders," Detective Medlock instigated.

Now she wasn't so confident. "What the hell are you two talking about?"

Detective Winters asked for a moment with his finger, then went inside his blazer and removed a manila folder. He could see Sabrina growing more tense with each passing moment. Then he finally retrieved the photos and held them out to her.

"We wanted to know what you were doing with 200 on these occasions?"

As Sabrina grabbed the photos, she started to shake her head. Obviously, these pigs must've confused her with somebody else. In the photos, 200 was caked up with this bright-skinned beauty who kinda reminded her of Nu-Nu from *ATL*. Just a cheaper version, if you asked her. Her face furrowed as she studied them further. They were at 200's spot. Out at a suburban home. At the airport. She handed the pictures back with the quickness.

"This ain't me," she said, her attitude evident.

"So, this ain't you…leaving the airport? "Detective Winters feigned ignorance. When he knew that this wasn't Sabrina all along. He was using an interview tactic that was designed to get her in her feelings, hoping that she would slip and tell them what they needed to know.

"Fuck an airport. Get those pictures out of my face. That's not me."

Detective Winters looked at the pictures then back over to Sabrina. He studied them again before his words came off rather concessively. "Well, my apologies. It's just that you two look so similar. And 200 has so many girls that it's been hard for us to keep up." There was some emotion in her eyes provoked by his petty words. But he had the look of a tiger in his, and now he was ready to pounce. "The bottom line is 200's name has come up in yet another pair of murders. And I know how much you want to protect him. But this is the only chance you'll get to clear your name and help us bring him to justice."

But Sabrina knew that she wasn't in trouble for anything. She began to slowly back up. "Why don't you go ask one of his other girls for help." She got inside her Camaro and slammed the door. Being around her son brought her comfort. But it didn't last long.

"Sabrina," she heard Detective Winters call through the window. "Jamel and JaMia Golliday didn't deserve this. This was an innocent girl, and you can help." He continued on about how she could reach him until her frustrations came to a boiling point.

"Just leave me alone, dang," she shooed them off. Once she saw the detectives retreating, she sank into her seat, exhausted with emotion. It was like seeing 200 with his other chick seem to open her emotional wounds. The lies, the betrayal, it was all hitting her at once. How could the man she knew turn into such a dog? A man who would play games when he said she could trust him. Someone who would creep, when she was supposed to be all he needed. This was the exact opposite of everything he promised, and that's what brought her to tears.

"Mommy, are you okay?" Lil Jason asked.

"I'm fine, baby," she said to protect him. But the truth was that Mommy was going through it. She couldn't figure out why 200 let it get to this point. They had a good thing going. This made absolutely no sense. She took a calming breath to clear her head. But it was like the thought of more of 200's bullshit kept elbowing its way through. Remembering the last argument they had when she told 200 to give her her money, she realized that he made no attempt to do that. Then she thought about the photo with him and ol girl at the airport. *But he was still out spending my bread on these random broads.*

Sabrina was seeing red right now, and her baby daddy was the reason. Suddenly, they didn't feel like family anymore. They felt like enemies. But even then, she almost allowed herself to make an excuse for him, thinking back on the man she fell in love with. But what kind of man would steal a hundred and fifty thousand from his girl when he was supposed to be the protector and provider for them? In her head, a callous, heartless one. And if that's how he wanted to be, then she had something for him.

Sabrina put a tight grip on the steering wheel and started the car. She did hear the detectives when they mentioned 200's name in the murders of the Golliday siblings. But she was so blinded by her own emotions that it took a little time to register. She backed out of the parking space and went to exit the lot. But her contemptuous mind was thinking, *I wonder what PG would do with this information?*

Chapter 24

Renee started hitting the Cabbage Patch as she stood under the Friday night lights and cheered on Jaylen at his football game. But she was wearing visitor's clothing in their crosstown rivals' section and really, she was out of pocket. "What are y'all lookin' at?" she sassed the sour faces before her face filled again with glee. "That's my baby out there. You go get 'em, boy."

Out of the seven games that Jaylen played, this was just the second one Renee attended. It was difficult at times for her to get around with this chronic pain. But her body was feeling fluid, so she made it a priority to come. Her cheers mellowed after their first-down play stalled. Then after the quarterback nearly threw a pick, she heeded the heckling fan's words and took a seat. She really wasn't paying the shade he was throwing any mind. She just wanted to grab her Sonic cup and take a sip of the Henn and Coke she snuck inside.

She relaxed in the seat and indulged as some of the home fans around her stood in anticipation of another big stop. But seeing Jaylen take the ball on a reverse, her cup found the ground and the mom found herself back on her feet. "Watch out," she warned him about the large linebacker in pursuit. Her voice was the most fervent of the fifteen thousand fans inside the new stadium. She watched with great tension. But Jaylen seemed to have it all under control, as he electrified the crowd with a juke move before leaving the defender in the dust. There was nothing but paydirt in front of him. He sprinted all the way to the house.

"Not again," a frustrated parent pouted. "They act like they can't stop him. It's his third touchdown of the day."

Renee was usually animated on his other scores. But this time, she was rather reserved. Seeing Jaylen kneeling on the ground and then pointing towards the sky, she knew he was dedicating this touchdown to his friend, Ju. "It's okay, baby," she said as her eyes became glassy and everything around her became obsolete. It was like all the grief he was feeling, she was feeling too. And she wanted him to know it was going to be okay. "You're alright, baby. Just keep your head up," she encouraged. She clapped lethargically before she fell back in her seat.

"That's a fine son you have," an older fan of the opposing team complimented.

"Thank you."

His kind words seemed to be the medicine she needed to get her vibe back on track.

As the fourth quarter began to wind down, the fans in the home section thinned out. The score had ballooned to 55 to 27, and most chose to get out of the parking lot to beat the traffic. Jaylen looked across the field and spotted his mom sporting their school colors proudly. "I'm right here," he read her lips. And when the game ended, he shook a few hands then made a beeline across the field. Renee had entered the field to meet him on the sideline. And noticing the sorrowful expression on his face, she opened her arms to embrace him. "C'mere, sweetheart," she said to the young prodigy as he latched onto her like a baby. Jaylen immediately began to cry into her collar. For him, the murder of his friend was downright devastating.

"It's okay what you're feeling, sweetheart. Let it all out." She rubbed his back. Many media outlets, seeing an opportunity, started to hustle in their direction to capture the scene. But Coach Phil stepped in and ushered them aside.

Renee saw the handsome chocolate man with the look of compassion in his eyes. He was wearing a polo shirt with the school logo on it. He must've been part of the team. "Thank you," she mouthed.

"Don't mention it. Is he okay?" Coach Phil asked. Then he thought that it may have been inappropriate that he interrupted. He took a subtle breath, then started over. "I'm sorry, I'm Phillip. But all the kids here call me Coach Phil. Jaylen, is everything okay, bud?" he asked while placing a caring hand on his shoulder. At the sight of his coach, Jaylen tried to toughen up.

"Yeah, I'm good," he said, but his voice broke.

"He's dealing with the murder of one of his close friends," Renee took the liberty of speaking up for him.

There was compassion in Coach Phil's tone.

"Sorry to hear that. But I'll bet he would be glad to see how hard you represented for him. Four touchdowns. 300 all-purpose. Boy, you really did your thing." Coach Phil heard a laugh escape Jaylen and continued to lay on the charm. "Not only that but look who's here. You got your mom here too." He whispered when he spoke to Renee. "He talks about you all the time." A reinvigorated Jaylen finally spoke up.

"Ma, this Coach Phil. You don't remember how I told you he was paying for the camps? The one who be gettin' me the shoes."

"Actually, I do now." She eyed Coach Phil. "And I'll be the first to say thank you."

"Thank me? Nah, don't worry about it, Mrs. Renee. Jaylen's a good kid. I'm just doing what I can to help."

Renee rested her weight on one hip and folded her arms as she watched the two make small talk. She could see Coach Phil took a great liking to her son. And from that, a respect for him was born.

Chapter 25

The clear blue waters relaxed Sabrina as PG took the beauty's hand and guided her to their oceanside sunbrella. This was their third day of a five-day trip to the remote island of Turks and Caicos. For Sabrina, this was PG making things right. For PG, this was a chance for him to clear his head. He's been torturing himself for the past few weeks, stressing about not finding his siblings' killer and reliving scenarios in his head as if it would make things undone. Lucky for him, he had something to take his mind off of that. And it came in the form of the baddie in the black Givenchy bathing suit, who had all the curves a man likes.

"This is nice," Sabrina gushed, stepping inside the luxury tent. It sat on a row with similar white tents, and she could see why PG had to shit that grip out just to get one. Two padded day beds, which faced the ocean, sat around a small makeshift fireplace that was built in the sand. There was also a section to drink and dine. While fine satin drapes offered seclusion from prying eyes and the bright sun. Sabrina loved how PG made this trip so romantic. It was like their sex game. Every day there was something different.

"So, am I out of your doghouse yet?" PG asked as he grabbed her waist and eased behind her. He was referring to how distant he'd been acting lately since his siblings' murders.

Sabrina turned around to face him. "Mmm...I guess."

"You guess? A nigga out here doing the most for you and all you gotta say is—I guess?"

"Boy, shut up with yo cute mad face. Of course, you're out of my doghouse—you were never in it." Her eyes softened and so it seemed her tone.

"It's just that whether you're up or down, I wanna have a chance to be there for you." PG took a step into her as he eyed her sexy lips. "So you down for me like that?"

"The way a real chick supposed to."

"You mean like all the way down?"

"Like fo' flats," she assured, wrapping her arms around his neck.

PG laughed then gave her a sweet smooch. And after going to the bar to pour up some tequila, he fell back on the daybed right next to Sabrina.

"You know this trip was about a little more to me than just spending some quality time with you. This was my brother Buck's favorite spot. And I even sent Mia and her friends out here after her high school graduation. So I guess—" his voice broke with emotion. It was clear it was difficult for him to talk about the subject. "—I guess it's like being here, I got a piece of them with me."

Sabrina saw the sadness in his eyes and grabbed his hand. "You got a piece of me too." She's been waiting for the right time to tell him that she was pregnant. And now that the opportunity was there, the words just seemed to flow. She grabbed his hand tighter. "I got some news that may lighten the mood."

"What kinda news?" PG grew curious.

"...I'm pregnant."

PG's face fell. "Pregnant like...pregnant?...pregnant?"

"Yep."

"No shit."

"And I'm bearing your child, too," Sabrina made that part known. She took his hand and placed it on the slight hardness of her stomach, then asked with an attractive smile, "See?"

"Man, I can't believe it. That's dope. We 'bout to have us a lil child." The news was better than PG expected. He was glowing like the Reunion Tower. "You can rest assured, I'ma hold it down and do everything I'm supposed to do. Fo'real, ma, that's on me. I ain't gon' be nothing like your bullshit ex."

Sabrina grew quiet as she repeated his words in her head. *I'm gonna be nothing like your bullshit ex.* And that he was. Over this past year, she tired herself wondering what it was that made 200 treat her this way. Until his blatant actions showed that he never gave a fuck about her. But fuck him. As far as she was concerned, everything they had was dead. Her allegiance was now to her new bae. She felt it was time she showed it.

"Umm," she said as if she was in deep thought.

"What? Are you not wanting to keep it?"

"No, it's nothing like that. It's just that I have something else to tell you. And you might want to relax a bit."

PG felt the gravity of her words and saw the seriousness in her eyes. It was like the whole vibe in their circumference changed. He repositioned himself on the daybed.

"Okay. Go 'head. What is it?" he asked.

"I think I know who killed your brother and sister."

PG spoke more authoritatively. "You think or you know?"

Now Sabrina was the one repositioning herself. The way he looked at her made her uneasy, almost in a fearful way.

"It's not what I think. It's what the police think," she spoke nervously. "They've been harassing me about everything that 200's doing. So when they mentioned his name in another double homicide, the Golliday name just stuck out."

PG became silent and it was hard for Sabrina to read him. But there was murder on his mind and he was anxious to get to it.

"So what you're telling me has truth to it, and I can take it for what it's worth?"

"Of course, PG. I know how much this means to you. I wouldn't play with you about no shit like this."

PG let out a deep sigh as he began to see carnage in his head with great clarity. He didn't know much about 200 other than what she told him. But he sure as hell was 'bout to find out.

***

PG took an emergency flight back to the Metroplex and left Sabrina to enjoy the rest of the trip. He had one thing and one thing only on his mind—to find this nigga 200 so he and the squad could handle up. He sat inside the office at his pallet recycling business, surrounded by a few of his men. These were the contacts he trusted to handle all his illicit dealings. They were how he was able to stay in the shadows and move like the average Joe. Studying him was McGraw, which was short for Quick Draw McGraw. His aggressive dark features and nappy fro made him appear as an average thug. But he was PG's well-paid chief of security and main enforcer. Maniacal to some, but a perfectionist at what he does.

To his left was Whitey, a red, pretty nigga. He was in charge of PG's out-of-state coke shipments and did just about any and everything that the situation called for. He was bouncing the name around on the tip of his tongue that his day-one nigga just dropped. He wanted to find the killer too. Buck and Mia were like family. "I'm tryna think of where I heard that name before," he pondered. "Just gimme a minute, it'll come to me."

Since 200's name seemed to be familiar to Whitey, PG was hanging on his every word. Then suddenly the doorknob twisted, getting their attention. And in walked the last man that they were waiting for, PG's uncle Slick. As always, Slick was living up to his moniker with his gray peacoat and matching dress slacks. The piercing glare of his eyes and shiny texture of his hair gave the elder Golliday a certain mystique. He was the one who set PG up with the plug. It was the least he could do after PG's father took a bullet for him.

"Sorry, I'm late. But I got here as soon as I could. Now tell me what was so important that made you have to cut your trip short."

"Unc, you ain't gon' believe this. But I found out the name of my peoples' killer."

The word "name" must've set off a light in Whitey's head because he started popping his fingers as if something was coming to him. "That's where I know that name from. That's that lil nigga out Highland Hills."

"You seen him around before?" PG asked, full of hope.

"Nah, can't say that I have. But I heard a lot about him. They say the lil nigga a fool. And he be runnin' 'round causing hell."

"Well that doesn't help me much," PG said, desperate for some answers. He felt that he could've pressed Sabrina for the rundown but didn't want to make her any more uncomfortable than she already was.

"But hold on, PG. It could. You see, I know all types of dudes out there. All I gotta do is throw a lil money around and they'll be tellin' me everything I wanna hear."

"Well, do that," PG suggested.

"No doubt, bro. That shit right there overstood."

"And in the meantime, I'll contact my colleagues in Internal Affairs to see what information they could gather," Slick told them. "This brother took two of ours. So there's no reason why him or his should be able to sleep."

Chapter 26

"C'mon back," Head told 200 as they made their way through the festive Shack. 200 figured it was because he had a play for him. But Head really wanted to lace him up.

The smell of smoke and strong cologne faded as they entered Head's pretentious office. And 200, comfortable in a gray Adidas pantsuit, took a seat on the edge of the desk and began to study the cameras. "Man, look at all the money floating out there," his tatted face formed a scowl. "What's up with the French Montana lookin' nigga by the fireplace? He look like he playin' with some change. Give me the rundown on him."

A condescending sigh left Head's nose as he looked at 200 and shook his head. "I see it's neva too much with you. I could'a sworn you just hit a lick on Buck for sumthin' like a million cash."

"Me...Buck. You got the wrong guy," he played dumb. When in fact, the reason why he wanted to a hit a lick right now was so he could quell his frustrations for not being able to find the Twinz.

"Well, that's not what I heard," Head looked at him skeptically. "Word on the street is you had yo hands in it. And you really might wanna watch yourself."

"What you mean?" 200 snapped.

"I mean exactly what I said. Them Golliday Boyz think you did it. And they been askin' around about you." When Head saw 200 stop to think, he added in a serious tone, "You should probably lay low for a minute. You might be in some trouble."

"Trouble," 200 scoffed. "Nigga, please. Trouble ain't lookin' for me. Niggas know what it is when it comes to 200. It's *Braveheart* on mines," he stood, becoming agitated.

"Calm down, my dude. I'm just the messenger," Head defended.

But he was delivering one that 200 wasn't tryna hear. "And you know the only message I'm tryna send is that I'm tryna get my cake up. So if anything comes up, just put me in rotation."

200 dapped Head up even though he was still fried out about the warning. He didn't want shit to get too awkward between them so he left while he had a chance. Stepping back through the house, rowdy shit talk rose from the dice games. But he quickly made his way out the front door of the pompous estate and into the cool of the night. He had a whole lot of shit on his mind, and figured the best thing for him to do was hit the pad and get some sleep.

***

In his bed back at the crib, 200 grew conscious of this weird dream he was having, then opened his beady eyes and began to look around the room. He saw that it was 7:05 am, too early for a night owl like himself. So he repositioned his head on the pillow and tried to fall back asleep. It's been said that answers to our problems come to us while we sleep. Well, if that's the case, he didn't know what to make of the dream he'd just had. It started with a grown Jaylen grieving at the NFL draft, then did a complete 180 to Renee studying broken glass in her driveway. Something told him that he should probably give the dream more thought. But he was feeling like, *fuck all this shit*. All he wanted to do was sleep.

200 laid in the bed tossing and turning for what seemed like just a few minutes. But when he opened his eyes and

looked at the clock, he was surprised to see three whole hours had passed. "Oh, shit. Let me get up," he said through parched lips. He didn't get up at seven but he damn sure didn't sleep all day. After some light yawning and stretching, he looked on the polished dresser for his breakfast. And there it was, a half-smoked blunt of that blueberry cookie. He eyed it like a bad chick, then fired that bad boy up. He hit the remote to his smart TV and the sounds of Lil Baby filled the air.

This seemed to be the beginning of a beautiful day. But it wasn't long before the weight of his problems filled his head. First it was the police, then his unresolved beef with the Twinz, old enemies, and now new ones like these Golliday Boyz that had Head so scared. But he was feeling like, *fuck them Golliday Boyz*. To him, they weren't any different than the other niggas that he fucked over. Just some new names on the list of people that wanted to see him dead.

He blew out a heavy stream of smoke while ashing the blunt, then fell back against the headboard where he seemed to relax. He had bigger problems on his hands as far as he was concerned. Like what he was gon' do about this home for his mom? Before the Twinz threw a wrench in his plans, he had it all figured out. He had one-twenty put to the side to go towards her house. And with the lick, it would have put him comfortably at the two-ten needed without having to dip in his stash. Now he was wondering if he should just buy a home with the loot he had. A thought that was accompanied by the unwelcoming feeling of what could happen if he didn't. Though he quickly curbed that but wasn't able to curb Head's warning.

You should probably lay low. You might be in some trouble. All this, however, seemed to run him hot because niggas was always talkin' about what they was gon' do and never wanted smoke. Moving his people was a priority, but he wasn't about to let that be the reason. It was his choice and he felt that when he moved his mom and Jaylen to a safer neighborhood, he had to do it up right. For the longest, he'd been plotting on the home with the large fireplace and vaulted ceilings. This the one his T-Jones deserved, and this was the one she was gon' get.

Chapter 27

The engine of Renee's dated Mazda sputtered before coming to life. It wasn't a problem that required mechanical service. Just a glitch that occurred sporadically since she owned the car. The problem was with these Indians and their funky little grocers. They wanna sell you inferior products then have an attitude for days. But she wasn't about to let one person ruin her day. She curbed him and all of his musty energy as she cut up her Jill Scott and started back home.

The only reason she was out to begin with was to get some ingredients to make her southwest chili. If it were up to her, she would have stayed in the house, it was too cold. But this was requested by Jaylen and she'd do anything for her baby. She didn't know why he was so enamored with her chili but he asked for it at least once a week. She was starting to brag it was where he got his strength.

After humming along to a few songs, she felt around her grocery bag for the bubble gum that she bought. That's when she touched her bell pepper and felt a perishable spot. She examined it closer. "Unt…uh. They charged me an arm and a leg for this." As she sat at the stop sign, she seriously contemplated going back. She even entertained how her vow to stop cursing might come to an end when she went back to the store. But then she looked at the misleading sun and thought about how close she was to home. It wouldn't have been worth the trouble to go back so she just went ahead to the crib.

She arrived in her familiar driveway minutes later, grabbed her bags and hurried into the house. "Woo, it's cold out there. That temperature dropping so fast. I hope I got everything 'cause I'm not coming back out the house." It was much cozier in here. But it was quiet enough to hear a pin drop. She was cutting the lights on when an odd sound reached her ear. It sounded like a bead hitting the floor, and it alarmed her for a minute. But she eventually ignored it and charged it to the mouse she'd seen the other day. She knew that she had to put more traps out before this became a problem. There hadn't been any mice since she'd been living there and there wasn't 'bout to be none now.

She got back to getting settled, starting with her coat, then her bags. It was going to make her proud to watch her baby throw down and she couldn't wait to get started. She took her groceries inside the kitchen then sat them on the counter. She had barely begun to wash her hands when a chill swept over her body. She paused and looked up, getting this eerie feeling. Then without warning, a gloved hand covered her mouth.

"Mmm! Mmm!" her muffled screams wailed as she went into a panic and tried to buck loose. But McGraw pinned her against the counter then whispered in her ear. He had his chrome in the small of her back, one in the chamber, ready to shoot. "Bitch, if you move again, I swear it'll be the last thing that you do." A tear left Renee's eye. What was he about to do?

***

200 was in the back of The Pinks Projects. He pulled close enough to his weed man's all-white Jeep to pluck the pick from out of his head. He always got two things when he came out here—strong weed and the inside scoop on the who's who of hustling. The weed man was just one of those guys who liked to talk about people's business. Sometimes 200

would act on it. But what he just said left 200's face like stone. 200 passed the money to him for the O he'd just copped then tried to get him to reveal more about what he just said.

"So these Twinz out here winning like that?" 200 feigned interest. His weed man had no idea that the trio was acquainted.

"Winning...sheit, they won. I heard they ran off on some West Texas connect. Now they tucked in New Orleans somewhere in some big ass mansion," he told his interpretation of the truth.

"Just parlayin,' huh?" 200 egged on.

"Like Big Meech. Them niggas throwing lavish parties with strippers and all that."

So far, 200 hadn't had any luck locating the Twinz or their people. But if he gave him something to act on he was gon' definitely get to it. He went for the gusto.

"Dang, they musta hit for some grip. Well, I hope they moved they family then. Cause I know if I was the opp, I'd be trying to hit everything crucial." But the response fell flat.

"I don't know if they did. But I know I would'a moved mine. That shit come with the game."

Seeing headlights appear in his Tahoe's rearview, 200 excused himself, "Let me get out of these folks' way. I'ma hit you when I need you."

200 hit his headlights as he blended in with the seven o'clock traffic. But it didn't take long for the conversation he had to pull him back in. *Mansions. Strippers. They really fucking off my money. That was supposed to be the money I used to move Renee into her new crib.* 200 was lost in his head now. For as much as he yearned to fuck them pussy ass Twinz off, a softer thought took over about Renee and the crib. He could almost hear her joy from being surprised with it and feel the satisfaction of watching her raise Jaylen there. He tried to call her earlier but she didn't answer. Figuring

since he was in the neighborhood, he decided to dip through to say hi and check in.

Around ten minutes later, gravel churned beneath his tires as he parked behind Renee's car. The first thing he noticed was that the fence was open which stuck out to him because Renee was religiously tidy about things around the crib. He was going to sit in the truck and roll up but he decided to do it in the living room instead.

200 shut the Tahoe's door then his steps gradually quickened because of the hawk's bite. He wasted no time retrieving the key and pushing his way inside. 200 shook his head. "That temperature dropping something else." After looking around and seeing most of the lights on he added, "T, it's just me." It surprised him that the TV wasn't on her show. But then again, she must be in here cooking. Jaylen would be home soon from his teenage activities and she always liked to make sure he had him a good meal.

Rubbing his hands in anticipation of what she may have whipped up, 200 walked his two-step to the kitchen. He saw the bag of groceries on the table and was about to ask her what she was finna cook, but stopped when an awful sight took the air out of his lungs. His shoulders rose as he fought an uphill battle for air. Giving into his legs and collapsing to the ground, his knees landed in a pool of blood. He didn't even know that he had began to survey Renee's body and examine her ample wounds. It all seemed unreal. Her multiple stab wounds. Unreal. The gunshot wound to the chest. Unreal. Him actually seeing his mother dead in her own home. Un-fucking-real.

200 was back on his feet without a clue about how he got there, pacing like he could walk for a thousand miles. He wanted to block everything out and say that this didn't happen. But no matter how hard he fought to turn back the hands of time, there she was. His T, his sweet T, right in the corner of his peripheral, dead. Pained tears began to cloud his vision. He still couldn't believe this. But before he could

look over and give his doubting mind the truth, he heard the front door squeak open and a few seconds later, Jaylen's voice.

"Ma...200. Where y'all at?"

Oh fuck. Jaylen. The body, 200 thought. He rushed to his feet then ran to the living room. He was clearly distraught when he looked at his brother, who appeared as if he had just come home from a date. But Jaylen paid his brother's appearance no mind and went on without a care.

"Dang, bro, I've been tryna get at you. I wanted to call you for a ride from the movies, but I messed around and lost my phone."

Then he noticed 200's troubled expression and what appeared to be blood on the left side of his leg. "Bro, what's going on? What happened?" 200 didn't know where to start, but his tears did it for him.

"Did something happen to Ma?" Jaylen took a step forward.

"You can't go in there," 200 braced him.

"What you mean I can't go in there?"

"It's just a lot to take in. And I can't let you see her, not while she's like this."

But Jaylen tried to persist. "Move...get out my way." The two brothers began to wrestle. The tears that were spilling from 200's eyes were now spilling from Jaylen's. He felt something tragic had happened and he was determined to find out what. "Bro, get off me," he whined, jockeying against him. "C'mon, man. Move."

200 was tussling with his younger brother with all he had. Jaylen was strong, but not strong enough to let him see this. The brothers continued their struggle. Jaylen wrestling to see what happened and 200 grappling to keep him from witnessing the gruesome scene. Ultimately, 200 won out as they fell to the ground with all of 200's weight on top of Jaylen.

"Let me up. Get off of me." Jaylen kicked like a child. The more he struggled with 200's weight, the more frustrated he grew. "Get off of me! Let me up!" He cried harder and louder.

His reaction brought more tears from 200 and he finally admitted, "She's dead."

"She's what?"

"She's dead, Jaylen."

A cry left the depths of his soul, but it wasn't loud. It was a low heartfelt pain. "Noohh...please tell me that you lying, Jason."

"I can't. I came to check on her and I found her like this. I wish I was lying too. Better yet, I wish I could've saved her." He wrapped his arms around his brother tighter.

They stayed on the ground in this position, both heaving into each other's shoulders, neither one willing the other to move. It seemed that they both were lost thinking about the special traits about their mother. The ones they would miss. And the ones they couldn't afford to lose. Finally, after literally twenty minutes on the ground, 200 grew strong enough to stand to his feet. He wasn't about to let his mother's body go without the proper respect she deserved. Shortly after, he ushered Jaylen to his feet.

"Look, can you please take my phone and go sit in the car?"

"Y–yes."

"I want you to call the police while I go pack everything that you need. You coming to stay with me."

Chapter 28

Three days later, at his apartment, aka the baby Ritz, 200 shifted through brochures for different funeral homes, then shook his head and threw them all on the ottoman. A deep sigh soon followed. He wasn't supposed to be planning a funeral, he was supposed to be covering his mother's eyes as he ushered her into her new house.

Damn, he dreaded how he didn't follow his intuition. Something kept telling him to take the one-twenty he had and buy her a home with that. But he was naive and wanted the home with the fireplace and vaulted ceilings. Now he and his brother were without the rock of the family and he was stuck dealing with the aftermath.

He grabbed two 'Percs off the glass table, took a sip of warm beer and threw them hoes back. Staying blowed had become his ritual over the past few days as he sat at home counseling Jaylen and tryna figure things out. Who would have done something like this? It could have been any number of enemies. Taj. The ése. Or maybe even G's people. But all the signs seemed to be pointed at the Golliday Boyz. They were the ones with the most incentive and ironically, Renee was shot dead in the kitchen just like Mia was. This was a time of great chaos and confusion for him. And since no one had exposed their hand, he really couldn't decipher who did what.

He pulled a half-smoked blunt of his favorite out of his joggers. Regardless of what he had going on, the weed seemed to always help him zone. But it did little to curb the restlessness inside his head. One minute he was ready to tear shit up. The next, he couldn't get the image of his beautiful mother out of his head. Why did I let this shit happen? His heart mourned. "I should'a moved them the minute that shit happened with Jaylen's boy, Ju. If not, then damn sho' after I hit that lick on Buck." He was so far gone that he hadn't realized that he was talking to himself. He caught himself when he heard Jaylen's sniffles as he entered the living room. The blunt had withered into nothing more than a long ash, so he sat it in the tray, then searched Jaylen's eyes and asked, "You okay?"

Jaylen hunched his shoulders as he plopped on the couch in his gray gym shorts and wife beater. "I don't know," he pouted. But 200 immediately knew what he was thinking when he began to stare into space.

"Thinking 'bout Ma again?" 200 asked, trying to get him to talk.

But all the losses he endured seemed to harden his young soul.

"Man, I don't know, bro. I'm thinking 'bout a lil bit of everything, honestly. Ma. Ju. Life. And I 've been giving some serious thought to quitting playing football."

"For what? You love football. Why would you do that?"

"I don't know," his voice quivered with pain. "I just don't feel like playing anymore." He covered his face and buried his head into a soft crevice and began to bawl.

200 darted across the couch and held his fragile body in his arms. "It's okay, Jaylen. You're just going through a lot right now. I understand. And I also understand you have a God-given gift….use it. Use it to the best of your ability. And when they ask why you go so hard, you tell 'em you do it for her." He sat Jaylen upright and pointed to his heart. "She's still with you, right here. Her love will always be there for you, so go out and make her proud."

The OG's words seemed to give Jaylen the strength he needed. He wiped his eyes.

"Jason, can I ask you something?"

"Anything."

"Is it okay if I go and stay with Coach Phil?"

"Coach Phil?"

"Yeah, me and his son are real tight. And he got this big ol home, and I'll feel much safer there." Jaylen held back on telling him how much Coach Phil said he was bad news, that he would do better distancing himself from him and even invited Jaylen to stay with him. But 200 was on the fence.

"I don't know about that shit," he shook his head. "Fo'real, I don't know." It felt like if he let Jaylen go stay with him, then everything he set out to do was a complete failure. He wasn't able to buy the home that he vowed to get for his mom and now the person he fought to have raised in a safer neighborhood didn't even feel safe with him. He sighed then pinched the bridge of his nose.

"What?" Jaylen asked.

"I'm just thinkin'," he told him as his mind began to reason. He didn't want to lose the thing he loved the most, but he damn sure didn't want his baby brother caught up in his beef. His enemies were real. Niggas made moves like this as a prelude before they got at you. And he didn't know where they were coming from, or from which direction they were going to hit next.

Then he was out on bond and had these open murder investigations, and at any time he could get taken off the streets. Just the other day, it was pure luck that the detectives who had it out for him didn't come by his mother's to do the report. But with all that's going on, who's to say when his luck would run out.

"So that's what you want to do?" he asked Jaylen as the idea began to grow on him.

"Yeah, I do. But it's not like I'm gon' stay there forever. I just want to be around my friend so he could help keep my mind off things."

"What? I can't help you keep yo mind off things?" 200 threw a couple of playful body shots.

"Nah, it ain't nuthin' like that. But you gon' be gone all the time. And at least I'll have somebody to keep up with me on the game. Then on top of that, when it comes to training, I'll have one of my coaches right there."

200 thought about the rapport that Coach Phil built with their mom. And he could see that in Jaylen's eyes he was more like Uncle Phil. "Fine. Give him a call." He passed Jaylen his phone.

A few seconds later, Jaylen was on the line with the Duncanville assistant. "Hey coach– this me. I got my brother here with me. Hold on for a second, he wants to talk to you."

"Yeah, Coach Phil. This is Jaylen's older brother, Jason."

"—Oh, I heard a lot about you."

"I heard a lot about you too. Jaylen told me that he's welcome to stay at your home?"

"That's correct."

"Well if he did, could you tell me what to expect while he stays?" They spent the next few minutes going over assurances like two protective parents. 200 thought Coach Phil was cool and got this vibe that they had known each other for some time. "We gon' have to meet," 200 suggested.

"We most certainly do. But I'm afraid it's gon' have to wait because I'm not in town right now. Though, as soon as I get back, I'ma make sure to get at you the first chance I get."

They went over some more particulars about Jaylen's stay. Then 200 ended the call and looked at the anticipation on Jaylen's face.

"What he say?" Jaylen asked impatiently.

200 stalled him out for a second because he wasn't too excited about what he had to say. "Pack your things," he

showed defeat. "I guess you're going to stay with your Coach Phil."

Chapter 29

200 grabbed the new iPhone that he got for Jaylen and sat it on his lap as he drove to Coach Phil's house. Jaylen wasn't lying. Coach Phil was doin' his best shit. He stayed in a beautiful, six-bedroom sanctuary where he paid more for the pool service and landscaping than most niggas did for rent. Jaylen said he got the home from investing in real estate. This made 200 think how he was gon' have to take some change and invest in real estate himself. He was sittin' on half a mil, not including the money he set aside to buy a house for Renee. Surely, he could take some change and make something shake.

200 entered the gated community then called Jaylen's friend's phone as he pulled in front of the earth toned estate. This was how the brothers had been communicating for the past few days, exactly how long it took for 200 to get burnt out with that. When Jaylen answered, he let him know he was outside.

"Cool," Jaylen said. "Let me throw on a shirt."

A few seconds later, 200 lit up watching Jaylen approach the truck. It was a natural reaction when he saw him, just from seeing the stages of his growth.

"You look better," 200 told him, which was more than he could say for himself. He couldn't seem to get over the fact that moving her could'a prevented his mother's death. Tie that in with the lingering questions he had about who may have killed her, then pour in some pressure from the Dallas

Homicide detectives, and you could see why he was so stressed.

But Jaylen brought some light during a time of duress. He responded to 200 with the natural charm that made him so likable. "You know it's easy for me to look better." He pinched his chin like he was that guy. "I'ma Goodwin, bro. Looks and stuff come honestly."

"Man, I wasn't talking 'bout those looks," 200 teased, peeping his lil swag. "While you over there thinking you Mackadocious or somebody." Jaylen was joking about how he might want to keep some of his girls close when 200 dabbed him on the elbow with something to get his attention.

"Here, I got you anotha' phone. It ain't much, but hopefully, you could make do."

Jaylen expected some lil run of the mill starter phone. But his brown skin beamed, seeing his new iPhone. "Wow. This mug is nice," he checked it out. "Big boy status. I can't wait to show Lil Craig so we could sit and download some games." Jaylen would've had this reaction whether it was expensive or not. One quality about him was that he was always grateful.

"Well, I'm glad you like it," 200 told him.

"Like it…shoot, I love it. These only been out for a couple of days. Coach Phil gon' be jealous when he sees this."

"Speaking of your coach, where he at?"

"Still out of town. Said he had to stay a lil longer. But I'll be sure to tell him you were asking when he gets back."

A moment passed as 200's high fell and he became distracted with his problems. He knew he needed to talk to Jaylen on a more serious note. His expression grew somber like a doctor prepared to give bad news.

"Say, I decided to leave the funeral arrangements up to Aunt Doonie. She's still deciding on who to let handle the service. But she believes the funeral will happen in no later than a week." It fucked 200 up to even say this. And he was expecting to see devastation from Jaylen. But when he looked in his eyes, he was surprisingly strong.

"Look, hang in there, bro. We gon' be alright, trust me." It was as if Jaylen had taken on 200's comforting brother role, especially when he playfully swiped his head. He chunked the deuce then ran in the house, excited to show off his new phone.

Well, I'm glad he's doing better, 200 thought. He put the Tahoe in drive then headed back towards the way. He had these warm sensations flowing through him, but upon thinking about Renee, his tatted face gradually fell to a scowl. He desperately wanted to find out who was responsible for murdering his mother. That's why he set up a meeting with Head, so he could learn more about the Golliday Boyz. True, he knew that he couldn't let the Twinz make it for that fuck shit they pulled. But when it all boiled down, his mother trumped everything.

Looking to the sky, 200 saw that it was filled with gray and there was no hint of sun. You couldn't even tell it was 4:00. He could sense that it was about to really pour down. But it seemed darker in his heart. He had murder on his mind.

He pushed through the congested traffic on the interstate. Then after passing the opulent downtown skyline, he finally made it to the hood. It was crazy to think that out of all the nice places he saw, the seven figure homes and a sprawling metropolis, he felt more comfortable here. Maybe because he knew he could let his pistol ride without fearing the consequences. The exact thing he planned to do when he found his mother's killer.

He pulled up to this lil rinky dink gas station. Most of the parking spots were filled, so he parked at the rear of the store. He needed to grab some blunts. He had all this animosity built up inside him. And the weed helped him control it long enough to make sure that he took it out on the right one.

Before hopping out of the truck, 200 checked his surroundings. Then, the minute his sneakers hit the ground he slid his hands inside his black letterman jacket. To avoid the cold? Nah. He was searching for the handle of that chrome. It gave him a little extra juice just knowing that it was there. He leisurely walked to the front of the store where he halted to avoid this woman who was arguing with someone on the phone. *Damn, no excuse me or nothin'*, he frowned. *You see, attitudes like that is why I don't go for ratchet hoes.* 200 was crazy enough as it is, and being with one of them toxic chicks was like a recipe for disaster—literally.

The doors to the store's entrance slid open. But 200 stopped when this woman by the gas pump made him do a double take. This was the type of double take you did when you liked what you saw. The slim hottie turned to the side a bit. Damn, she got ass too. *Now, that's what I go for,* he smirked, taking a detour towards her silver Volvo Jetta. As he eyed her, her angel eyes got stuck on him like she was eyeing him too.

"Lemme get that for you," he insisted, offering to pump her gas.

The woman's fair skin turned flush. "Nooo...I think I'm doin' just fine."

"Well, I wish I could say the same." 200's face playfully saddened as the hottie showed concern.

"Why...what's wrong?"

"Nothin'. Just feel like you 'bout to leave before I get your name and number and that would be messed up."

"Well, as the old saying goes, you can't miss what you neva had."

200 couldn't resist the opportunity to shoot a sexual slug out there. "See, that's what I'm tryna work on."

"Boy," she said, responding to his boldness.

"Nah, fo'real. You got me feeling like I ran into an old friend and we got some catching up to do. So, where you wanna go?"

She responded with the same boldness he did when he threw his slug out there. "Try Ruth Chris, then the Galleria."

"That's cool wit me. And maybe we could even add the Hyatt to that list."

The beauty laughed. "You wish." And they continued to vibe. For two people who'd just met, they really got each other's personality.

"I was just playin' about Ruth Chris and the Galleria and all that. I was really tryna run you off. But I see you, Mr. Persistent."

"Don't trip, Devan. If those the places you like they just became my favorite spots too." He hung her gas pump up for her, then hit her with a lil charm before asking for her number. As she entered it, a lone raindrop hit her. But it was followed by another. Then another one. And before they knew it, the clouds began to catch steam.

"Awl, my hair," she pouted girlishly. "Jason, let me go before it really starts to pour down." She told him that was her number calling and to save it. Then, she hopped in her Jetta and smashed out.

200 felt a couple drops hit him and threw his hood over his knotted fade. He was so busy trying to run in and out the store that he didn't even see the blacked-out Range Rover that pulled in front of him. "Shit," he said, stopping to avoid walking into the truck. The truck paused in front of him long enough for him to see his reflection. Then it drove off without incident. But it still left a stain. He could've sworn it felt like the occupants were eyeing him. But he couldn't even see inside the truck. Maybe, he was just being 'noid.

A large man who was leaving the store kept the door open for him. And he stepped inside and stood in what appeared to be the shortest line. But a woman kept protesting to the clerk about how she wanted to exchange a damaged product. *C'mon*, he silently urged as he heard the raindrops splattering against the top of the building. Then the rain began to turn up, falling with the force of hail.

"Look, I got it. I'll pay for a new one. And while you at it, get me a box of cigarillos," he told the clerk. The woman had a look on her face like she still wasn't satisfied. But all he wanted to do was get some blunts and get the hell out of dodge. "Thank you," he told the clerk when he came back with the blunts. He took the box and slid them in his pocket, but before he made his exit, he stopped and zipped his coat.

"Damn," he said, looking out the store at the storm. It was raining cats and dogs. It was hard to even see out in front of you. He contemplated waiting in the store until the brunt of the storm passed. But instead, he took a deep breath then courageously went out.

"Shit," he said, as the cool drops quickly drenched his clothes. His jeans felt like he dived in a pool, making him think he probably should have stayed in the store. But it was too late to turn back now. He was mere meters from his truck. A few swift steps later, the big body started to appear. And he was about to hit the alarm before an attacker's boot surprisingly crashed into the small of his back.

"What the—" he started to say as he practically flipped up off the curb. The velocity sent him crashing to the ground, but only for an instant. Like a real-life commando, he turned and drew iron before it was kicked from his hand. And now he was fucked.

"Stay still, pussy," a masked extendo holder told him. And as 200 looked around, it seemed more gunmen appeared. They had those crazy killer eyes and wore disguises that barely hid their faces. You could see one of their noses, *one's dark skin*. But the one quality you saw in all of them was they weren't fuckin' around. A man who wore a purple scarf over his face, picked up 200's loose gun, then gave it to the supposed ringleader. After sliding it in his pocket, his menacing voice boomed.

"Now get your bitch ass up. You 'bout to take a ride with us." He leveled his pistol at 200's peripheral and nodded towards the blacked-out Range Rover behind him.

200 laughed. "Get in the truck? Nigga, you got me fucked up. You might as well shoot me right now. Otherwise, I ain't budging."

"Shoot you? Nah…" Now he was the one who laughed. "That'll be too easy. How 'bout we shoot yo lil brutha instead?" He tossed a familiar-looking blue Samsung on 200's lap.

"What's this?"

"That's yo brutha's old phone. I know he probably wondering what happened to it. And if you don't get in that truck, you gon' be wondering what happened to him."

200 hesitated in thought.

"Or should I make the call?"

200 could feel in his heart that he meant every word. But could they really get to his brother? He couldn't afford to find out. He hustled to his feet.

"Nah, you ain't gotta do that. I'll get in the truck. Just stand down and chill," 200 placated.

"Smart man. I would hate to have to kill the lil homie. He got such a promising future. Know what I mean?"

The only thing 200 knew was that if he had the ups on him, he would'a been domed his bitch ass. He was lucky the shoe wasn't on the other foot. Angrily, he clenched his jaw when one of the goons gripped his arm and forced him towards the truck as if he was tryna handle him. He had gotten so used to being the one doing the hunting that he never thought the day would come when he would be the hunted. They abruptly stopped in front of the Range and the ringleader began to frisk him.

"You won't be needing these," he said, then tossed the keys to 200's Tahoe to one of the guys. "C'mon," he gripped 200's arm again. This shit was getting old. 200 sorta resisted until being pushed in the back. "You hard of hearing, Tough Tony. Get yo bitch ass in the truck."

Normally, 200 would've went all out before he let some niggas chump him but he had to think about Jaylen. He couldn't let a hair on his head get touched. He complied and got in the Range. And just like that, they were in traffic with his Tahoe trailing.

Inside the truck, everyone seemed to be focused and on a mission. The faces in the front row went about business as usual, but the two that sandwiched him in the middle were ready to pop shit off. There was also a goon sitting behind him holding his pistol in place. Whoeva this squad was, they weren't taking any chances.

"Man, what's this?" 200 asked. "How'd y'all get my brother's phone?" His question made the ringleader to the right feel like he was doing too much.

"Man who asked him to talk? Did you ask him, PG?" He looked at the guy in the driver's seat."

"Nah, I ain't ask him shit."

"That's what I thought. Keep yo muthafuckin mouth closed or say one more thing and I'ma silence it for good."

Do it for Jaylen…Jaylen. He reminded himself. But with all the disrespect, it was easier said than done. He wanted to turn the tables so bad that he could practically see the carnage of what would've happened if he did. *The lunging for the exposed weapon. The truck swerving. The satisfying gun blast.* But what would happen to Jaylen if he did? When the unbidden prospect rose in his mind, it also produced a word…exactly. He shook his head and sighed roughly from his nose, as he decided to fall back and take one for the team.

The rest of the trip was gravely quiet with minimal noise coming from the raindrops and splashes of water underneath the tires. As 200 busied himself looking past the raindrops on the windshield, he noticed the scenery change to that of a commercial district. From the looks of the dated buildings, you could tell this area once boomed. But it was now desolate and destitute, a mere remnant of itself. They pulled behind the gate that said, "Keep Out" and in front of a large building that used to be a warehouse. You could feel a shift in the energy when the truck was thrown in park and as if in unison all the doors flew open.

"Get out," the ringleader told him.

Get out, 200 repeated cynically, sighing as he scooted behind the goon to get out the truck. But his feet barely stood on the muddy gravel long enough to make an impression. He was quickly accosted to the middle of both trucks, where they sat in a semicircle with the headlights on. A man with dark skin and a bushy beard approached 200. His eyes were glued on him, and he had an air of cockiness in his step.

"Do you know who I am?" PG pointed to his chest.

200 processed the distinct scar over his eye, his wavy hair, and his bushy beard.

"Actually, I don't."

"Well, how 'bout Buck or Mia? Do those names ring a bell?"

The mention of PG's siblings brought a flash of suspicion to 200's eyes. But he shook his head with bewilderment.

"Ain't coming to you yet? Well, I wouldn't want to remember neither especially if I felt like answering 'yeah' could get me kilt. But those are two names that I'll neva forget 'cause they were my brother and sister. And that money you took from them— that was mine."

PG's words forecasted trouble, like a siren hittin' the hood. But 200 didn't get to where he was by folding. All he knew was…deny…deny…deny.

"Look, I ain't got nothin to do with that, fam. I'ont know nothin about your siblings…who you are…why I'm here…yo money…or none of that peeps."

But his words fell flat like a rock hitting a wall. Evidently, PG knew something that 200 didn't.

"Say, you could pass a lie detector test right now and it wouldn't matter to me. That's what this is and this is how it's gon' go," PG laid the law down. "I came here to kill you, but I decided to give you an option. Something that'll give you a chance at better days." He grew a devious smile. "You can give me my money back, all one point two-five mil, or you and yo brother gon' be dealt the same fate I dealt your mother."

"My mother?" 200 asked in shock.

"Yeah, your mother. You didn't think it was a coincidence that your mother was killed like my beautiful sister, Mia was. Did you?"

200 lost it. My mother? He couldn't get to PG, so he took off on the closest dude to him, clocking him in the jaw with a tight fist. He continued to punch into the crowd with reckless abandon. Fuck their guns. Fuck the fact that he was outnumbered. These niggas killed his mother. He was going for broke. Another wild punch whistled through the air and caught the dude wearing the purple scarf dead in the nose. He had his eyes out for PG the whole time. But before he could get to him, a hard barreling punch blindsided him in the temple. Wop! Momentarily, he lost consciousness. Then a round of kicks from the goons to his collapsed body began to snap and crack him back to.

"I'ight, don't kill him," he heard PG's distinct voice. But McGraw was going so hard that he had to run over and grab him.

"Chill, baby boi. You gon' fuck around and kill him before we get the loot."

After PG made sure McGraw was calm, he stared down at a woozy 200. He had no sympathy for the nigga. He looked at him then tossed the keys to his Tahoe on his chest. "Wake up, bitch nigga. One point two-five ain't gon' bag itself." He kicked him a little just to help him come to. "All that money you took, I need that shit back ASAP. Otherwise, pick some plots on that ground for you and yo brother. 'Cause that's where I'ma bury both of y'all. Starting with him first."

When the door closed, 200 opened his eyes in time to hear one more taunt. "And keep yo phone nearby," PG yelled out the window. "We'll be in touch."

If 200 wasn't awake, he woke up when splatters of mud hit his pant leg. Apparently, he was still punch drunk. But he was coherent enough to get the gist of PG's threat. *I need all my money back ASAP. Otherwise, I'm killing you and yo brother. Starting with him first.* PG's distinct voice resonated with him like a broken record. *Starting with him first... starting with him first.* He tried to convince himself that this wasn't happening. But the fact remained that his brother's life was on the line, unless he could get that money.

200 sat up and grunted from the pain in his side. He tasted blood in his mouth and felt a slight trickle from his nose. It was a low point for him, sitting in the rain at this empty factory on his dick. But he had no time to sulk. He had to put that money together. "Agh," he groaned as he tried to push himself off the ground. His first attempt was futile. But after affirming that he was good, he got to his feet on the second go.

As 200 approached the Tahoe, he noticed that his clothes were sullied, and stripped down to his hoop gear and threw the rest in the truck. Not long after he was kicking up gravel and leaving the factory, starting his thirty-minute trip to get to his spot. He drove like a bat out of hell, cutting in and out of traffic, doing well over the speed limit. He might as well have been a cop. But he had his own emergency of sorts. Like if he didn't get PG his one and a quarter mil, his promising brother, Jaylen, was gon' end up dead.

200 knew that he had roughly six hundred thou to his name, but where was he gonna get the rest? And exactly how long was ASAP supposed to mean? He sighed roughly from his nose thinking about his predicament. Shit was all fucked up. The death of his mother, now this. He didn't even know if PG would hold up to his end of the bargain once he gave him the cash. But he did know that if the Twinz wouldn't have crossed him, he would have never been in this position. He would have moved his mom and maybe she would still be alive. This made him wanna kill them pussy ass niggas all

the more. That thought consumed him as he headed back towards his spot.

***

Looking in the vanity mirror in his master bedroom, 200 noticed a few red scuff marks and scrapes. There was even a clot forming in his left eye. But nothing he couldn't fade. He gargled some water then spit out blood in the sink. And as he was about to throw some water on his face, he heard his phone vibrate.

Bzzzz...Bzzzz

For a second, he debated if he should acknowledge it. Then he thought about PG's warning and went ahead and glanced at the screen. He saw it was Queen, which he had her number saved under "Boss B." He decided to read the text.

–Just thinkin' bout U. Wanna let U know that I'm here 4 U in NEway I can be

The text ended with a flirty emoji which put a crack in the stone around his heart. *It's kinda good to know that her pretty ass was thinkin' 'bout a nigga,* he thought. Maybe she meant it when she said that she was really down for me. But he would entertain that later. Right now, he was fully focused on getting this money to PG to ensure Jaylen's safety.

He lowered his face under the faucet, then splashed it with some water. But the refreshing round did little to distract him from his problems. In fact, by the time he looked in the mirror, his problems only seemed to magnify. There was stress on his face where confidence usually reigned. Worry storming through the pupils of his dilated eyes. But this wasn't how it was supposed to be. Not for a nigga like him. Not for the goon the streets knew as, 200.

When the summer first started, he went from turning up on these niggas to turning up with what he called a purpose. *Maybe I can take some of this money and put it to use*, he'd reasoned, *like buying a house for moms in the 'burbs so Jaylen would be insulated from the ills of the streets.* Unconsciously for 200, Jaylen's success was his success. It gave him a chance to see what his childhood would be like had his dopefiend father not robbed him of his. He always knew he was a bright kid with athletic promise. Now he was determined to give Jaylen something he didn't get—the best chance at living out his dreams.

But although a good heart was an attribute of his, as well as jackin' shit, he was flawed when it came to seeing how his actions affected others. He had an ego problem. If he jacked you, he felt like, "Yeah nigga, I did it." And any nigga that's fucked up about it could get it in slugs. But a nigga did and now he was mourning something that was irreplaceable. Immeasurable. And her beautiful name was Renee. "Fuck," he spewed, bringing his fist down on the light-colored sink. There was no more T-Jones' house to go to. No more Sunday dinners. No more of that loving smile. "I should have moved her when I had the chance." He rested against the sink. His eyes were dry. But he had tears pouring inside.

The big question now was, if he had the chance to hit the same lick for over a million cash, would he do it all over again? The old him would have answered "Yeah" in a heartbeat. I would'a just moved my family sooner. But the new him would answer with an emphatic, "No." I could never put my family under the gun like that. Neva. Neva. Neva. To his credit, he'd grown in that respect. But PG 'nem didn't give a damn about his change, claiming that if he didn't come up with the money, they were gon' kill Jaylen.

The thought made his jaw clench. He looked in the mirror again and saw the condition of a man that was ready to go out of his mind. What the fuck these niggas think? Like I ain't a young legend with that toolie. Like my murda game ain't supreme. And I won't bust they mufuckin heads. But bad as he wanted to go to war, he couldn't. He was learning to think of how his actions affect others and the most important thing was getting Jaylen out of this situation.

Conceding, he splashed some more water on his face, then took a deep breath from the back of his lungs. The situation wasn't all bad. He wasn't sold that PG could get to Jaylen. For all he knew, he was just applying pressure to get the money. But Jaylen was ducked off in this big safe house far away from the hood. And that was basically his goal from the get-go. Right? Accepting this consolation, he found himself enjoying the prospect of Jaylen living up to his potential promise. Excelling in school. Graduating from college and doing what he was ordained to do, play in the NFL. This made a smile sprout on his face.

Then his phone vibrated, snapping him out of his daze.

Bzzzz...Bzzzz

Look Queen, I know you mean well but now ain't a good time. If you knew about all this shit I had going on, then you would definitely understand. 200 assumed it was her texting him. He was prepared to quiet the alert. When he peeped the strange number, his face screwed up. "773...what kinda area code is that?"

Then the text slowly scrolled and with each passing word, alarm rose inside of him.

On second thought, do I really need the money?

There was a picture attachment which 200 opened and saw Jaylen with a cape on at the barbershop getting his haircut. He didn't know if the picture was as recent as today or if it was old. Man, how in the fuck did they get this? 200 thought. And how did they get my number?

Fretting that his brother was in danger, 200 ran in the living room, found Jaylen's new number and punched it in. But he was so nervous and jittery that the phone slipped from his hand. It took him multiple tries to calm his nerves, but he was finally able to complete the call. Holding his breath for a response, he listened anxiously. And with each passing moment, he got the sense that something was terribly wrong.

"C'mon, bro. Pick up," he urged.

He didn't know if Jaylen had been kidnapped or was alive. He just needed to hear that he was okay. The phone continued to ring. Suddenly he heard a pause, but it was only Jaylen's annoying voicemail picking up.

"Jaylen, where you at, lil bro? I ain't get you that phone for nuthin'. Pick up the muthafucka and put it to use."

200 immediately called the phone right back. And after the third ring, his deepening anxiety quelled.

"Hello."

200 breathed laboriously as if he'd run a mile. Then he tried to steady his voice as he spoke to the receiver.

"Jaylen...you alright?"

Jaylen was confused by his worried state.

"Umm...yeah. I'm good, bro. You?"

"Yeah, I'm better now. But don't pay that shit no mind, I just wanted to hear your voice. What's up with you?"

"Nothing really. Just chillin'. 'Bout to get at Lil Craig in this game."

His voice was too warm for him to be in any danger and after realizing he was at Coach Phil's, he started to relax.

"Yeah, play him. Stay in your lane. 'Cause messin' wit me, you already know what's gon' happen."

"Man, whateva. You ain't got nothing. You my light weight. And you know anytime you want it, I'll serve you up."

200 felt at ease vibin' with Jaylen. But he knew this was something that wasn't guaranteed.

"Y'all have fun playing the game. But I want you to know that I love you, bro." 200 felt that he had said it in passing, so he made sure to reiterate. "Nah, fo'real. I love you, Jaylen. And I mean that shit to the grave. For as long as I'm alive, I'll do everything in my power to make sure you straight. You hear me?"

"Yeah, I hear you. And I love you too," Jaylen said, but he began to whisper to a male voice in the background. 200

waited patiently as the conversation ensued. But he called out to him when he sensed some worry in his tone. "Jaylen, you iight?"

Jaylen didn't respond, but 200 could hear a tad more of his brother's voice. It sounded like somebody was whispering right in his ear.

200 began to worry. "Jaylen," he called with more vigor. But still, no response. In fact, Jaylen's voice grew more distant. He listened closer with great attention and could only hear bits and pieces of the conversation. But he heard a lot of ruffling. Followed by a deathly silence. Then after a long pause, he heard the worst possible sound.

B'ough!

"What the fuck!" 200 grew confused. "Jaylen!" he called desperately. He held the phone as close as he could to his ear. But all he heard was more ruffling until he eventually heard nothing. Looking at the screen he saw that the call was dead. He dialed Jaylen's number back but got no answer.

He flailed his arms. "Lord please tell me ain't nothing happen to my brother?" His heart cracked, writhing with pain at the prospect. It was amazing he was even able to stand because it was like the weight of the world had hit him all at once. He took a few listless steps, digging in what little hair he had on his head. He didn't know if he should call Jaylen again or just go by Coach Phil's house to see what's what.

But his hands seemingly decided for him as he looked at the phone and noticed he'd pressed talk. As he listened for an answer, he was on edge like a defendant who was waiting on a jury to return a verdict. He had never been this attentive to anything in his life.

Ring…Ring

An unwelcome thought entered 200's mind long enough to make him feel dread. He profusely shook his head to reject the thought.

Ring…Ring

200 began to pretend that it wasn't a gunshot he heard. That his brother was fine and that could have been something that fell and made that sound.

Ring...Ring

In the span of a few seconds, as he sensed the call would end, his fears amplified. It was like not answering was the worst news of any news. "Please... Please...Please don't let nothing have happened to Jaylen. They already took my moms. He's all I got."

He heard a slight pause like somebody picked up, but it was only Jaylen's annoying voicemail again.

Finally, he just said, "Fuck it," and ran to grab the Drake-O. The unwelcome thoughts tried to re-enter his mind but he shook his head, fighting them off. "Fuck that, Jaylen iight," he affirmed with great conviction. He was gon' keep on telling himself that until he started to believe it. Entering his bedroom closet, he went straight for the top shelf. "There that bad boy go," he said to himself. "Might as well gon' grab the extra clip too. 'Cause them pussies gon' bleed about playin' with mines."

When he came back in the living room, he was moving so fast that his shin clipped the chic table. Surely, it would leave a mark. But it didn't slow his stride one bit. He was too busy focusing on the pain he was about to inflict. He grabbed his keys and went for the door without even bothering to put on any more clothes. These niggas had better hope his brother was straight. Otherwise, he was about to bring *World War III* right here to Dallas.

To be continued...

GET IT IN SLUGS 2
Coming Soon

About The Author

B. Stall is a big connoisseur of urban fiction and hopes to bring the visibility to it that reflects the urban community's impact in other areas of culture.

GET IT IN SLUGS | B. STALL

Lock Down Publications and Ca$h Presents Assisted Publishing Packages

BASIC PACKAGE $499 Editing Cover Design Formatting	UPGRADED PACKAGE $800 Typing Editing Cover Design Formatting
ADVANCE PACKAGE $1,200 Typing Editing Cover Design Formatting Copyright registration Proofreading Upload book to Amazon	LDP SUPREME PACKAGE $1,500 Typing Editing Cover Design Formatting Copyright registration Proofreading Set up Amazon account Upload book to Amazon Advertise on LDP, Amazon and Facebook Page

***Other services available upon request.
Additional charges may apply

Lock Down Publications
P.O. Box 944
Stockbridge, GA 30281-9998
Phone: 470 303-9761

Submission Guideline

Submit the first three chapters of your completed manuscript to ldpsubmissions@gmail.com. In the subject line add **Your Book's Title**. The manuscript must be in a Word Doc file and sent as an attachment. Document should be in Times New Roman, double spaced, and in size 12 font. Also, provide your synopsis and full contact information. If sending multiple submissions, they must each be in a separate email.

Have a story but no way to send it electronically? You can still submit to LDP/Ca$h Presents. Send in the first three chapters, written or typed, of your completed manuscript to:

LDP: Submissions Dept
P.O. Box 944
Stockbridge, GA 30281-9998

DO NOT send original manuscript. Must be a duplicate. Provide your synopsis and a cover letter containing your full contact information.

Thanks for considering LDP and Ca$h Presents.

NEW RELEASES

BLOODLINE OF A SAVAGE 1&2
THESE VICIOUS STREETS 1&2
RELENTLESS GOON
RELENTLESS GOON 2
BY PRINCE A. TAUHID

THE BUTTERFLY MAFIA 1-3
BY FUMIYA PAYNE

A THUG'S STREET PRINCESS 1&2
BY MEESHA

CITY OF SMOKE 2
BY MOLOTTI

STEPPERS 1,2&3
THE REAL BADDIES OF CHI-RAQ
BY KING RIO

THE LANE 1&2
BY KEN-KEN SPENCE

THUG OF SPADES 1&2
LOVE IN THE TRENCHES 2
CORNER BOYS
BY COREY ROBINSON

TIL DEATH 3
BY ARYANNA

THE BIRTH OF A GANGSTER 4
BY DELMONT PLAYER

PRODUCT OF THE STREETS 1&2
BY DEMOND "MONEY" ANDERSON

NO TIME FOR ERROR
BY KEESE

MONEY HUNGRY DEMONS
BY TRANAY ADAMS

Coming Soon from Lock Down Publications/Ca$h Presents

IF YOU CROSS ME ONCE 6
ANGEL V
By Anthony Fields

IMMA DIE BOUT MINE 5
By Aryanna

A THUGS STREET PRINCESS 3
By Meesha

PRODUCT OF THE STREETS 3
By Demond Money Anderson

CORNER BOYS 2
By Corey Robinson

THE MURDER QUEENS 6&7
By Michael Gallon

CITY OF SMOKE 3
By Molotti

CONFESSIONS OF A DOPE BOY
By Nicholas Lock

THA TAKEOVER
By Keith Chandler

BETRAYAL OF A G 2
By Ray Vinci

CRIME BOSS
By Playa Ray

Available Now

RESTRAINING ORDER 1 & 2
By **CA$H & Coffee**

LOVE KNOWS NO BOUNDARIES 1-3
By **Coffee**

RAISED AS A GOON I, II, III & IV
BRED BY THE SLUMS I, II, III
BLAST FOR ME I & II
ROTTEN TO THE CORE I II III
A BRONX TALE I, II, III
DUFFLE BAG CARTEL I II III IV V VI
HEARTLESS GOON I II III IV V
A SAVAGE DOPEBOY I II
DRUG LORDS I II III
CUTTHROAT MAFIA I II
KING OF THE TRENCHES
By **Ghost**

LAY IT DOWN I & II
LAST OF A DYING BREED I II
BLOOD STAINS OF A SHOTTA I & II III
By **Jamaica**

LOYAL TO THE GAME I II III
LIFE OF SIN I, II III
By **TJ & Jelissa**

IF LOVING HIM IS WRONG...I & II
LOVE ME EVEN WHEN IT HURTS I II III
By **Jelissa**

PUSH IT TO THE LIMIT
By **Bre' Hayes**

GET IT IN SLUGS | B. STALL

BLOODY COMMAS I & II
SKI MASK CARTEL I, II & III
KING OF NEW YORK I II, III IV V
RISE TO POWER I II III
COKE KINGS I II III IV V
BORN HEARTLESS I II III IV
KING OF THE TRAP I II
By **T.J. Edwards**

WHEN THE STREETS CLAP BACK I & II III
THE HEART OF A SAVAGE I II III IV
MONEY MAFIA I II
LOYAL TO THE SOIL I II III
By **Jibril Williams**

A DISTINGUISHED THUG STOLE MY HEART I II & III
LOVE SHOULDN'T HURT I II III IV
RENEGADE BOYS 1-4
PAID IN KARMA 1-3
SAVAGE STORMS 1-3
AN UNFORESEEN LOVE 1-3
BABY, I'M WINTERTIME COLD 1-3
A THUG'S STREET PRINCESS 1&2
By **Meesha**

A GANGSTER'S CODE 1-3
A GANGSTER'S SYN 1-3
THE SAVAGE LIFE 1-3
CHAINED TO THE STREETS 1-3
BLOOD ON THE MONEY 1-3
A GANGSTA'S PAIN 1-3
BEAUTIFUL LIES AND UGLY TRUTHS
CHURCH IN THESE STREETS
By **J-Blunt**

CUM FOR ME 1-8
An LDP Erotica Collaboration

GET IT IN SLUGS | B. STALL

BLOOD OF A BOSS 1-5
SHADOWS OF THE GAME
TRAP BASTARD
By **Askari**

THE STREETS BLEED MURDER 1-3
THE HEART OF A GANGSTA 1-3
By **Jerry Jackson**

WHEN A GOOD GIRL GOES BAD
By **Adrienne**

THE COST OF LOYALTY 1-3
By **Kweli**

BRIDE OF A HUSTLA 1-3
THE FETTI GIRLS 1-3
CORRUPTED BY A GANGSTA 1-4
BLINDED BY HIS LOVE
THE PRICE YOU PAY FOR LOVE 1-3
DOPE GIRL MAGIC 1-3
By **Destiny Skai**

A KINGPIN'S AMBITION
A KINGPIN'S AMBITION II
I MURDER FOR THE DOUGH
By **Ambitious**

TRUE SAVAGE 1-7
DOPE BOY MAGIC 1-3
MIDNIGHT CARTEL 1-3
CITY OF KINGZ 1&2
NIGHTMARE ON SILENT AVE
THE PLUG OF LIL MEXICO 1&2
CLASSIC CITY
By **Chris Green**

GET IT IN SLUGS | B. STALL

A GANGSTER'S REVENGE 1-4
THE BOSS MAN'S DAUGHTERS 1-5
A SAVAGE LOVE 1&2
BAE BELONGS TO ME 1&2
A HUSTLER'S DECEIT 1-3
WHAT BAD BITCHES DO 1-3
SOUL OF A MONSTER 1-3
KILL ZONE
A DOPE BOY'S QUEEN 1-3
TIL DEATH 1-3
IMMA DIE BOUT MINE 1-4
By **Aryanna**

A DOPEBOY'S PRAYER
By **Eddie "Wolf" Lee**

THE KING CARTEL 1-3
By **Frank Gresham**

THESE NIGGAS AIN'T LOYAL 1-3
By **Nikki Tee**

GANGSTA SHYT 1-3
By **CATO**

THE ULTIMATE BETRAYAL
By **Phoenix**

BOSS'N UP 1-3
By **Royal Nicole**

I LOVE YOU TO DEATH
By **Destiny J**

I RIDE FOR MY HITTA
I STILL RIDE FOR MY HITTA
By **Misty Holt**

GET IT IN SLUGS | B. STALL

LOVE & CHASIN' PAPER
By **Qay Crockett**

TO DIE IN VAIN
SINS OF A HUSTLA
By **ASAD**

BROOKLYN HUSTLAZ
By **Boogsy Morina**

BROOKLYN ON LOCK 1 & 2
By **Sonovia**

GANGSTA CITY
By **Teddy Duke**

A DRUG KING AND HIS DIAMOND 1-3
A DOPEMAN'S RICHES
HER MAN, MINE'S TOO 1&2
CASH MONEY HO'S
THE WIFEY I USED TO BE 1&2
PRETTY GIRLS DO NASTY THINGS
By **Nicole Goosby**

LIPSTICK KILLAH 1-3
CRIME OF PASSION 1-3
FRIEND OR FOE 1-3
By **Mimi**

TRAPHOUSE KING 1-3
KINGPIN KILLAZ 1-3
STREET KINGS 1&2
PAID IN BLOOD 1&2
CARTEL KILLAZ 1-3
DOPE GODS 1&2
By **Hood Rich**

THE STREETS ARE CALLING
By **Duquie Wilson**

GET IT IN SLUGS | B. STALL

STEADY MOBBN' 1-3
THE STREETS STAINED MY SOUL 1-3
By **Marcellus Allen**

WHO SHOT YA 1-3
SON OF A DOPE FIEND 1-4
HEAVEN GOT A GHETTO 1&2
SKI MASK MONEY 1&2
By **Renta**

GORILLAZ IN THE BAY 1-4
TEARS OF A GANGSTA 1/&2
3X KRAZY 1&2
STRAIGHT BEAST MODE 1&2
By **DE'KARI**

TRIGGADALE 1-3
MURDA WAS THE CASE 1-3
By **Elijah R. Freeman**

SLAUGHTER GANG 1-3
RUTHLESS HEART 1-3
By **Willie Slaughter**

GOD BLESS THE TRAPPERS 1-3
THESE SCANDALOUS STREETS 1-3
FEAR MY GANGSTA 1-5
THESE STREETS DON'T LOVE NOBODY 1-2
BURY ME A G 1-5
A GANGSTA'S EMPIRE 1-4
THE DOPEMAN'S BODYGAURD 1&2
THE REALEST KILLAZ 1-3
THE LAST OF THE OGS 1-3
By **Tranay Adams**

MARRIED TO A BOSS 1-3
By **Destiny Skai & Chris Green**

GET IT IN SLUGS | B. STALL

KINGZ OF THE GAME 1-7
CRIME BOSS 1-3
By **Playa Ray**

FUK SHYT
By **Blakk Diamond**

DON'T F#CK WITH MY HEART 1&2
By **Linnea**

ADDICTED TO THE DRAMA 1-3
IN THE ARM OF HIS BOSS
By **Jamila**

LOYALTY AIN'T PROMISED 1&2
By **Keith Williams**

YAYO 1-4
A SHOOTER'S AMBITION 1&2
BRED IN THE GAME
By **S. Allen**

TRAP GOD 1-3
RICH $AVAGE 1-3
MONEY IN THE GRAVE 1-3
CARTEL MONEY
By **Martell Troublesome Bolden**

FOREVER GANGSTA 1&2
GLOCKS ON SATIN SHEETS 1&2
By **Adrian Dulan**

TOE TAGZ 1-4
LEVELS TO THIS SHYT 1&2
IT'S JUST ME AND YOU
By **Ah'Million**

GET IT IN SLUGS | B. STALL

KINGPIN DREAMS 1-3
RAN OFF ON DA PLUG
By **Paper Boi Rari**

THE STREETS MADE ME 1-3
By **Larry D. Wright**

CONFESSIONS OF A GANGSTA 1-4
CONFESSIONS OF A JACKBOY 1-3
CONFESSIONS OF A HITMAN
By **Nicholas Lock**

I'M NOTHING WITHOUT HIS LOVE
SINS OF A THUG
TO THE THUG I LOVED BEFORE
A GANGSTA SAVED XMAS
IN A HUSTLER I TRUST
By **Monet Dragun**

QUIET MONEY 1-3
THUG LIFE 1-3
EXTENDED CLIP 1&2
A GANGSTA'S PARADISE
By **Trai'Quan**

CAUGHT UP IN THE LIFE 1-3
THE STREETS NEVER LET GO 1-3
By **Robert Baptiste**

NEW TO THE GAME 1-3
MONEY, MURDER & MEMORIES 1-3
By **Malik D. Rice**

CREAM 2-3
THE STREETS WILL TALK
By **Yolanda Moore**

THE STREETS WILL NEVER CLOSE 1-3
By **K'ajji**

GET IT IN SLUGS | B. STALL

LIFE OF A SAVAGE 1-4
A GANGSTA'S QUR'AN 1-4
MURDA SEASON 1-3
GANGLAND CARTEL 1-3
CHI'RAQ GANGSTAS 1-4
KILLERS ON ELM STREET 1-3
JACK BOYZ N DA BRONX 1-3
A DOPEBOY'S DREAM 1-3
JACK BOYS VS DOPE BOYS 1-3
COKE GIRLZ
COKE BOYS
SOSA GANG 1&2
BRONX SAVAGES
BODYMORE KINGPINS
BLOOD OF A GOON
By **Romell Tukes**

CONCRETE KILLA 1-3
VICIOUS LOYALTY 1-3
By **Kingpen**

THE ULTIMATE SACRIFICE 1-6
KHADIFI
IF YOU CROSS ME ONCE 1-3
ANGEL 1-4
IN THE BLINK OF AN EYE
By **Anthony Fields**

THE LIFE OF A HOOD STAR
By **Ca$h & Rashia Wilson**

NIGHTMARES OF A HUSTLA 1-3
BLOOD AND GAMES 1&2
By **King Dream**

GHOST MOB
By **Stilloan Robinson**

GET IT IN SLUGS | B. STALL

HARD AND RUTHLESS 1&2
MOB TOWN 251
THE BILLIONAIRE BENTLEYS 1-3
REAL G'S MOVE IN SILENCE
By **Von Diesel**

MOB TIES 1-7
SOUL OF A HUSTLER, HEART OF A KILLER 1-3
GORILLAZ IN THE TRENCHES
By **SayNoMore**

BODYMORE MURDERLAND 1-3
THE BIRTH OF A GANGSTER 1-4
By **Delmont Player**

FOR THE LOVE OF A BOSS 1&2
By **C. D. Blue**

KILLA KOUNTY 1-5
By **Khufu**

MOBBED UP 1-4
THE BRICK MAN 1-5
THE COCAINE PRINCESS 1-10
STEPPERS 1-3
SUPER GREMLIN 1-4
By **King Rio**

MONEY GAME 1&2
By **Smoove Dolla**

A GANGSTA'S KARMA 1-4
By **FLAME**

KING OF THE TRENCHES 1-3
By **GHOST & TRANAY ADAMS**

GET IT IN SLUGS | B. STALL

QUEEN OF THE ZOO 1&2
By **Black Migo**

GRIMEY WAYS 1-3
BETRAYAL OF A G
By **Ray Vinci**

XMAS WITH AN ATL SHOOTER
By **Ca$h & Destiny Skai**

KING KILLA 1&2
By **Vincent "Vitto" Holloway**

BETRAYAL OF A THUG 1&2
By **Fre$h**

THE MURDER QUEENS 1-5
By **Michael Gallon**

FOR THE LOVE OF BLOOD 1-4
By **Jamel Mitchell**

HOOD CONSIGLIERE 1&2
NO TIME FOR ERROR
By **Keese**

PROTÉGÉ OF A LEGEND 1&2
LOVE IN THE TRENCHES 1&2
By **Corey Robinson**

THE PLUG'S RUTHLESS DAUGHTER
By **Tony Daniels**

BORN IN THE GRAVE 1-3
CRIME PAYS
By **Self Made Tay**

MOAN IN MY MOUTH
By **XTASY**

GET IT IN SLUGS | B. STALL

TORN BETWEEN A GANGSTER AND A GENTLEMAN
By **J-BLUNT & Miss Kim**

LOYALTY IS EVERYTHING 1-3
CITY OF SMOKE 1&2
By **Molotti**

HERE TODAY GONE TOMORROW 1&2
By **Fly Rock**

WOMEN LIE MEN LIE 1-4
FIFTY SHADES OF SNOW 1-3
STACK BEFORE YOU SPLURGE
GIRLS FALL LIKE DOMINOES
NAÏVE TO THE STREETS
By **ROY MILLIGAN**

PILLOW PRINCESS
By **S. Hawkins**

THE BUTTERFLY MAFIA 1-3
SALUTE MY SAVAGERY 1&2
By **Fumiya Payne**

THE LANE 1&2
By **Ken-Ken Spence**

THE PUSSY TRAP 1-5
By **Nene Capri**

DIRTY DNA
By **Blaque**

SANCTIFIED AND HORNY
by **XTASY**

BOOKS BY LDP'S CEO, CA$H

TRUST IN NO MAN
TRUST IN NO MAN 2
TRUST IN NO MAN 3
BONDED BY BLOOD
SHORTY GOT A THUG
THUGS CRY
THUGS CRY 2
THUGS CRY 3
TRUST NO BITCH
TRUST NO BITCH 2
TRUST NO BITCH 3
TIL MY CASKET DROPS
RESTRAINING ORDER
RESTRAINING ORDER 2
IN LOVE WITH A CONVICT
LIFE OF A HOOD STAR
XMAS WITH AN ATL SHOOTER

Printed in the USA
CPSIA information can be obtained
at www.ICGtesting.com
CBHW061221171124
17514CB00005B/108